HOT
SEAL

A *HOSTILE OPERATIONS TEAM* Novella

LYNN RAYE

NEW YORK TIMES & USA TODAY BESTSELLING AUTHOR

HARRIS

www.**lynnrayeharris**.com

First Edition: August 2015
Library of Congress Cataloging-in-Publication Data

Harris, Lynn Raye
    Hot SEAL / Lynn Raye Harris – 1st ed
        ISBN-13: 978-1-941002-09-4

1. Hot SEAL—Fiction
2. Fiction—Romance
3. Fiction—Contemporary Romance

OTHER BOOKS IN
THE *HOSTILE OPERATIONS TEAM* SERIES

PROLOGUE

Five years ago…

IVY MOANED AS A HAND skimmed over her bare skin, coming to rest on her breast. Long fingers toyed with her nipple, sent instant lust rocketing through her core. She could hardly believe they'd already made love twice in the past few hours and she was still ready for more.

"Dane," she whispered as he turned her in his arms and sucked her nipple into his mouth. His tongue slid around the peak, teasing, tormenting, before he let her go and moved on to the other breast.

"You're beautiful, Ivy," he said, rising up to settle himself between her legs. "So fucking beautiful. And you're mine."

He plunged into her body then, and she wrapped her arms around him, her heart filling with love and a kind of desperation that frightened her in some ways. Dane was too intense, too big and overwhelming to her senses.

And she loved him beyond reason.

His body took hers to heights she'd never experienced

with anyone else. He elicited the kind of cries from her that would have been embarrassing if she'd thought about it from an objective point of view.

More, Dane... Harder, Dane... Fuck me, Dane...

Each time, he responded with exactly what she needed. His mouth took hers possessively, demanding surrender. She gave it to him. Gave herself to him. Wrapped herself around him as he rocked into her, as her body caught fire, as she tumbled over the edge with a sharp cry.

He came immediately after she did, and then he gathered her to him and rolled until she was cradled against his hard chest.

"So what's it like being married to me so far?" he asked in a whisper.

Her heart thumped. *Married.* They were married now, had been for all of about twelve hours. She caressed the damp muscles of his chest. "Heavenly. Best decision I ever made."

"Even if you were drunk during the ceremony?"

Ivy laughed. "Not quite drunk. Just tipsy. And so were you, I might add."

He laughed too. "The dangers of Vegas, I guess."

Ivy pushed herself upright to gaze down into Dane's stunning blue eyes. A splinter of doubt gnawed at her, like always. Happiness wasn't something she was accustomed to. In her experience, it wasn't something that lasted for long.

It was spring break and they were still in college, though graduation was only a couple of months away. They were starting the next phase of their lives a little early, but it was okay. It *would* be okay.

"You don't regret it, do you?" she asked.

His gaze softened and he reached up to brush her hair back from her face. "No. Do you?"

Ivy shook her head. "Absolutely not."

When she dropped her gaze, Dane tipped her chin up with his finger. "What's wrong, honey?"

"Aren't you a little worried about what your parents might say?"

Dane's eyes chilled. "I don't care what they say. It's my life, not theirs."

She knew that his parents were a sore spot with him, but she'd never quite understood why. He came from a family where he'd gotten the best of everything, while she'd been bounced from foster home to foster home from the time she was eight years old. Eventually she'd ended up with her grandmother—her dad's mother—but Beth McGill hadn't had much to give her other than a grandmother's love. Which had meant everything to her.

"Okay, baby," she said. "I just don't want them to hate me."

Dane looked fierce. "They won't. How could they? You're perfect."

Ivy's heart thumped painfully. Dane was the only person in the world besides her grandmother who'd ever said she was perfect. She wasn't, of course.

"I love you, Dane."

He grinned and pulled her down for a kiss. "I know, honey. I love you too. Nothing can change that."

ONE

THE SUBMARINE WAS GONE. DEA agent Ivy McGill stood in the jungle with her team, listening to the *whop-whop-whop* of helicopter rotors as they beat the air nearby. They'd gotten the satellite imagery a few hours ago, and they'd busted ass to get out here in order to confiscate the sub and capture the workers. She hadn't kidded herself that the drug lords who'd commissioned the damn thing would be here, but she'd hoped to at least get a worker who would talk.

All she'd needed was one. But there were no workers either. There were only bodies and the smell of burning rubber and spent gunpowder.

The jungle had been turned into a shipyard, amazingly, with living quarters for fifty or sixty men and workshops to build submarines. There were generators, gas stoves for cooking, and storage racks for marine parts. There was also a narrow estuary where presumably subs

1

would be piloted out of the jungle and into the river beyond. From there, the subs would be taken to a port and loaded with cocaine before making the journey north to the United States.

"Middle of the fucking jungle," Ace Martin said, coming up beside her. "How'd they build a fucking submarine in the middle of a jungle?"

"With a lot of money," Ivy told her partner, her gaze poring over the abandoned shipyard.

Their information indicated there was only one submarine at the moment, with more commissioned to be built, but it represented a step up in design from the usual homemade fiberglass subs the drug runners used. The new sub was steel, fitted with Chinese engines, powered by lead-acid batteries, and capable of traveling for ten days without refueling. It could submerge to a depth that rendered it silent to the US Navy—and it could hold three tons of cocaine.

That was a lot of fucking cocaine hitting the streets of the United States.

A Colombian soldier shouted something, and Ivy took off at a run. Ace was right behind her. They skidded into one of the workshops to find a soldier pointing a gun at a grease-stained man who held his hands high and begged the soldier not to shoot.

"Are there others?" Ivy asked the soldier in Spanish.

"No," he told her. "Just this one."

She spoke to the man, told him not to fear them. But his eyes were wide as he darted his gaze between her, Ace, and the soldier. Outside, the shouts of other soldiers and DEA agents carried through the jungle.

"What happened here?" she asked the man.

All he did was repeat his plea not to shoot. Ivy wanted to growl in frustration, but instead she went over and handcuffed him. Then she told the soldier to lower the gun. He did, and she jerked her head at Ace.

"Get this one on a chopper. I want to talk to him when we get back to HQ."

"Aye, aye, captain."

Ivy frowned. "Very funny with the nautical stuff."

Ace grinned and walked over to collect the worker. Ivy marched back into the jungle. The humidity was thick out here, and the stench from the nearby mangroves was strong. Men moved through the shipyard, searching for any signs of life.

Unfortunately, there was no one else alive. Whatever had happened out here, it hadn't been pretty. It wasn't unlike the Ruiz family to turn against the people who had helped put them where they were, but it didn't make a whole lot of sense to kill everyone. These were the workers who'd built the sub. They were skilled men, recruited from the shipyards and navies of South and Central American countries. It took a lot of time and money to assemble this kind of crew. It made no sense to kill them, especially since getting the men out would have been far easier than getting the sub out. Hell, the way the thing was built, you could fill it with men and sail away.

So why the slaughter?

Ivy shuddered as she raised her gaze to the sky. That was what she didn't understand about these bastards. What she could never understand. They killed when they didn't have to. Because they could.

Ivy took one last look around before she headed for the chopper. She had work to do, and time was running out.

"You want to do what?"

Dane "Viking" Erikson stared at the two men standing across from him. He'd been training with his men at the Virginia Beach facility when he'd been summoned to this meeting. He hadn't thought much of it at the time, but right now he was staring at an admiral in white and an Army colonel in desert camouflage and wondering what they'd been smoking.

The colonel—Mendez was his name—was the one to speak. "I need a SEAL team, Lieutenant. Your name came up as the one to lead it."

"For the Hostile Operations Team." Dane shook his head. "I thought that was a myth. Just a tale the Army guys told when they were feeling inferior."

Mendez snorted. "Not a myth. And not strictly Army anymore either. HOT is joint service, and the SEALs are the next step. We've got a state-of-the-art facility in Maryland and more money than you can imagine. The missions are critical to national security, and their scope is widening. We need you." Mendez glanced at Admiral Carter.

The admiral's mouth was a grim line. "You're the best fit, Dane."

Dane's gut tightened. "Because my dad is General Erikson, you mean."

Mendez nodded. "Doesn't hurt. You know the Army.

Understand it."

"I joined the Navy. I'm not interested in the Army. *Sir*."

Mendez's look could best be described as disgusted. For some reason, that made Dane feel contrite. He cleared his throat and stared at the wall behind the colonel's head, not liking that this man could reduce him to feeling like a puny child in his father's home.

Just like old times.

Mendez's tone, when he spoke again, was conversational. But Dane didn't kid himself that the man was as mild mannered as he appeared. No, there was steel in that tone and steel in his eyes.

"So you don't care for the Army. I don't much care for the Navy. But here's the thing, son. We're in this together. We're fighting for the same goddamn thing, and if I need a SEAL team on my roster, I'm getting one. You can come willingly, or you can come with a grudge. Your choice. But you *are* coming. So pack your gear and get your ass up to Maryland. I'll expect you at oh seven hundred the day after tomorrow. Any questions?"

"What about my team?"

"They'll get their orders. In the meantime, you can come and get cozy with us while you wait. We won't hurt you, I promise."

Dane wanted to say something sarcastic. He very wisely didn't. The colonel was yanking his chain at this point. He'd set himself up for it, so he could hardly blame the man. "Yes, sir."

"Excellent." The colonel pulled his cap from his belt as he turned toward the door. "Welcome to HOT, Lieutenant Erikson. We hope you enjoy the ride."

TWO

THE COLONEL HADN'T BEEN KIDDING that the facility was state of the art. It took about half the morning to get clearance, a Common Access Card, and all the codes and various protocols needed to enter and exit on his own power, but finally Dane had everything and found himself in a locker room staring at a group of faces that looked at him curiously. There was no hostility, which he found encouraging.

"You the frogman?" one of the dudes asked.

"You the ground pounder?" Dane returned.

One of the other guys snorted. "Yeah, that's Iceman all right. He pounds the ground pretty regularly. When he's not pounding a certain senator's daughter."

"Shut up, fuckhead," the one named Iceman growled. "That's my fiancée you're talking about."

"Sorry, Ice. Couldn't resist."

"You'd better be sorry or I'll pound your face for you. Then what, pretty boy?"

Dane turned away and opened the locker he'd been assigned. All his gear was there. He didn't know what the hell he was supposed to do with any of it while here, but he supposed Colonel Mendez would waste no time in letting him know.

"Hey, frogman, we didn't mean to insult you or anything," the second guy said, and Dane turned around again.

The man walked over and held out his hand. "Chase Daniels. Welcome to HOT."

Dane eyed the guy for a second before he gripped the offered hand. "Dane Erikson."

They engaged in that age-old ritual guys have of squeezing the daylights out of each other before they let go again.

The other guys in the room stood and came over to thrust out hands. After introductions and handshakes all around, the bones in Dane's hand felt decidedly bruised. He couldn't tell if they'd done it on purpose or if they were being nice. Though he nearly laughed to think of a roomful of Special Ops warriors being nice.

But they were a brotherhood, even if they were different services. SEALs worked with other services on operations. Dane had worked with Delta Force, Marine Force Recon, Air Force PJs, the CIA, ATF, and DEA in the past.

But he'd never worked with HOT. Hell, he hadn't thought they existed. If Delta Force was the Army's secretive arm, then HOT was their invisible one. The guys just didn't exist.

Except they did, because he was standing here with them. Idly, he wondered if his father knew. General Erikson had been an Airborne Ranger back in the day. He worked at the Pentagon now, doing God knew what since Dane rarely spoke to him.

In fact, he didn't particularly like being within close

driving distance of the old man. Not that he felt compelled to visit or anything. Their relationship was best when carried out over the phone.

But his mother would expect him, and he could hardly refuse her. He drew the line at regular Sunday dinners, though he'd have to show up for a couple here and there.

He didn't plan on informing his parents of his new assignment for as long as possible. For all he knew, it wouldn't last anyway. He'd piss this colonel off, and he'd be bounced back to Virginia Beach before he could count to ten.

Hell, he kind of hoped that was the case. Except, fuck, he was definitely curious now that he was here. This facility was equipped with stuff he'd thought was still in the testing phase, and the gear was more than a little bit interesting. He at least wanted to be here long enough to explore.

"Colonel wants us," a man said, peeking his head into the room.

Everyone dropped what they were doing and headed for the door. Dane wasn't planning to go, but then Chase stopped and looked at him.

"He means you too."

Dane shut his locker and trailed after the group of men walking down the hallway. They passed into a big conference room and took seats around a table. There was a whiteboard on one wall and a projector overhead.

Dane took a seat in a leather chair just about the time someone shot to attention. The rest of the men followed suit. Dane automatically joined them as Colonel Mendez walked into the room.

"At ease," he said, and they sank back down on their

chairs. His gaze landed on Dane.

"We're glad you could join us, Lieutenant." Mendez opened up the laptop sitting at the head of the table and tapped some keys. "We have an interesting situation in Colombia. Our Navy man should be particularly fascinated."

Dane glanced at the others. There were puzzled looks on a few faces as the whiteboard flashed to life.

A satellite shot of a jungle appeared on-screen. There were white-roofed buildings spread out around the area and a fence around the perimeter. Drug runners, probably.

There was also a curl of dark water winding through the jungle near the compound. And then Mendez zoomed in and revealed an object in a small clearing. It was big, torpedo-shaped—

Dane stood before he realized he'd done so. All eyes turned to him. The colonel was watching him with an uplifted brow.

"What do you see here?"

Dane moved closer, studying the object. He'd heard of these things, but this one was bigger than was typical. Yet it was what it was.

"I see a submarine, sir."

Mendez nodded. "That's right. Intel indicated there was only one of them finished, but another was in the process of being built." He pressed a button and a new slide flashed up on the screen. This one contained specs for the submarine. Specs that chilled Dane. This wasn't your typical floating coffin the drug runners used. This was something different.

"Sir," Dane said, and the colonel looked at him. He cleared his throat. "Isn't this the kind of thing the Navy usually deals with?"

Or the DEA since the damn thing belonged to drug runners. He hated thinking about the DEA because that inevitably brought thoughts of his ex-wife, but this was exactly the kind of thing they would be interested in.

"Typically, yes." The colonel brought up another slide. "But here's the reason we're involved."

This picture was of bodies strewn about the compound. The next picture showed a wrecked shipyard with charred debris—and no sign of the finished sub. There was another sub form, but it was clearly in the process of being built.

"We've had intel indicating the Freedom Force is pursuing a plan to make a dirty bomb and detonate it somewhere on the Eastern Seaboard. That's not anything new. But then we received information two weeks ago that said they were in active negotiations with the Ruiz family to have them build a sub. There was supposed to be a meeting, an exchange of money—but it seems our friends from Qu'rim were impatient after being taken to inspect the equipment. They ambushed the makeshift shipyard and absconded with the finished sub."

"Fuck me," one of the other guys said.

Another cleared his throat. This one was the officer in charge of the team. Matt "Richie Rich" Girard.

"So the Freedom Force wants to detonate a dirty bomb on the Eastern Seaboard—and now they have the delivery system to get by our defenses."

"The Navy will find that thing," Dane said. "It can't be that difficult. Set up a dragnet and go after them."

The colonel shook his head. "You'd think that, wouldn't you? But you saw the specs."

He pulled up another slide, this one an analysis of the capabilities of the sub.

Silent... Submergible to a depth of eighteen hundred feet... ten days without refueling... could render radar detection useless... highly dangerous as a method of infiltration into US waters...

A chill ran down Dane's spine. If the damn sub was undetectable to the Navy, that wasn't a good thing at all.

"It gets worse," Mendez said. "The DEA traced the sub to Cartagena, where a dockworker reported seeing something being loaded onto a sub like this one. What he saw wasn't a dirty bomb. It was a little too big for that— and it fits the description of a warhead the Russians can't seem to locate."

THREE

MIGUEL ANTONIO RUIZ WAS NOT a happy man. His fingers toyed with the rim of his shot glass. He'd already downed two shots of the finest American whiskey, but he was not feeling in the least appeased.

"We are going to find that bitch," he said to no one in particular. His lieutenant, Juan Ortega, stood by silently. He knew better than to talk. "And we are going to make her pay."

Miguel snapped his fingers, and Juan obediently came over with the bottle. Miguel emptied the shot and Juan poured another.

Miguel was tired of the DEA getting all up in his shit. Sure, his submarine had been stolen by someone else—someone he'd let into his little jungle shipyard—but he knew where they'd gotten their information. The Americans had given it to them, most specifically one Special Agent McGill. That bitch had been a thorn in his side for the past couple of years.

He'd tried to buy her off—subtly, of course—but she wasn't corruptible. It was like she had a specific grudge against all things Ruiz. Which, he supposed, she probably did.

It had taken him a long time to find out the truth about her because it had been buried so deep—too deep for even the DEA to find, it seemed.

She was Maya's kid. Little Maya. He hadn't thought of her in years. She'd betrayed him, betrayed the family, when she'd run away to America with her sailor man.

That hadn't worked out, however, and she'd come crawling back. He picked up the shot glass and sniffed the liquor. His taste buds tingled with anticipation.

He hadn't meant for her to die. He'd only meant for her to pay.

Miguel shrugged. Shit happened. It was not his fault.

Maya hadn't needed to die, but her kid... that one was living on borrowed time. She was like a starving dog with a bone. She simply wouldn't let go. She had a grudge because she knew the truth, and she would do anything she could to get to him. She was taunting him.

He picked up his phone and replayed the footage of her standing in his shipyard, wisps of smoke rising into the air around her, her long dark hair whipping in the breeze. Her mouth was a flat line and her eyes were grim.

He recognized that look. It was determination and a need for revenge all rolled into one. She wouldn't let go of the bone. She would follow him to the ends of the earth to get what she wanted, which was the utter ruin of his business.

He couldn't let that happen.

The door burst open and Sergio strode in. He threw his hands wide. "What the fuck, Miguel? They took our sub."

"I know, brother."

"We need to get it back. That shit cost a lot of money."

"I'm working on it."

Sergio threw himself down in a chair and flicked a hand at Juan. Juan retrieved another shot glass and poured a drink.

"How are you working on it?"

"Ivy McGill."

Sergio blinked. "What does she have to do with this? We should be thanking our lucky saints *she* didn't get the sub. If the Americans had taken it, we'd never see it again."

Miguel snorted. "You're blind, Sergio. Don't you see? She didn't trust her government to move fast enough, so she gave the information to the thieves. Now that they have it, she will move to confiscate it in open water."

Sergio shook his head. "That makes no sense. She landed in the jungle with a team only hours after it was stolen. Why would she do that if she already knew it was gone?"

Miguel waved a hand as if shooing away a particularly bothersome bug. "I don't know her thoughts, but I know she was behind it."

Because she was too determined, too obsessed, not to be. He could feel it in his bones. And his bones never lied.

"Then what do you propose to do?"

Miguel studied the fresh liquid in his glass. He was feeling better now. Warm inside. It had taken time to get this far, but he had a plan.

"I know how to find her now. Soon she will be dealt with."

Ivy strode into DEA headquarters and went straight for her boss's office. Leslie Webb's secretary didn't even blink as Ivy walked past and entered the room.

Leslie looked up from her paperwork, one eyebrow arched, as Ivy closed the door behind her.

"Been expecting you, Special Agent McGill."

Ivy sucked in a breath. She'd worked herself into a good lather on the way over here, but she needed to be cool and calm or she wouldn't get anywhere. "Ma'am, respectfully, this is bullshit. I don't want the military taking this away from us. We've worked too hard to bring down the Ruiz family and their network."

"Ivy, you have to think about this." Leslie sat back and gave her the once-over. "This is out of my hands. There are terrorists involved, and that trumps everything. The Ruizes will still be there when this is over. The military isn't taking this away from us permanently. But they have to be involved now."

Ivy scrubbed a hand down her jacket and sank into a chair across from Leslie. It infuriated her that the military had taken over, and yet she knew there was no changing it.

"All right, fine. But I want to be involved. At least send Ace and me in to advise them, or whatever we need to do. Don't let us be cut out of this."

One corner of Leslie's mouth twitched. "Do you know why I'm sitting here and you're over there?"

"Because you've been here longer and have more experience?"

"That's right, Ivy. Not only that, but this isn't my first rodeo." She picked up a piece of paper and handed it over. "You're in. Get your ass over to Maryland—and don't let those special operator motherfuckers forget who found the damn sub in the first place, all right?"

Triumph surged in her as Ivy shot to her feet and smiled. "Yes, ma'am."

She hurried from Leslie's office and found Ace, who was sitting at his desk and looking fierce as he flipped through the tabs on his computer screen. Ivy waved the paper, and Ace lifted an eyebrow.

"Want to go to Maryland with me? We're paying a visit to the military."

Ace grinned as he stood and grabbed his jacket. "Fuck yeah, darlin'. Let's roll."

The drive to Maryland didn't take too long. Getting into the facility where the military had headquartered the submarine hunt took a bit longer. Ivy was steaming by the time she and Ace were stripped of all their technology and then read in to the super-secret military program before being led behind the thick walls and yards of razor wire. Eventually, they were shown in to see an Army colonel in camouflage who looked far more imposing behind his desk than he should for a man sitting down. He had salt-and-pepper hair, which at first glance made him seem older than he likely was—but his face was only lightly creased around the eyes. It was a handsome face, with a strong jaw and piercing dark eyes that had a way of boring into you.

He leaned back and gave them both the once-over. "Welcome to the Hostile Operations Team, Special Agent McGill. Special Agent Martin. I understand you're here to observe my team as we work to locate this sub you found in Columbia?"

Ivy tried not to let her hackles rise, but it was damn hard not to. Ace had been in the military once, so he was far better at this kind of thing than she was. Not to mention she'd once had the pleasure of an Army general looking down his nose at her as if she weren't good enough for his son.

Which, in General Erikson's mind, she hadn't been.

"That's right, sir. We're here to observe and advise," Ace said.

Ivy very wisely kept her mouth shut. The DEA had found the damn sub, and they were the ones who worked to keep drugs out of this country. These guys... Well, she knew what they did was important, but they didn't know the first thing about the Ruizes—or how drugs could destroy a family without anyone being a user.

The colonel got to his feet and came around his desk. He was as big and imposing as she'd expected a special-ops soldier would be. If he appeared in a Hollywood action film tomorrow, she somehow wouldn't be surprised. He looked the part.

He leaned back against the desk and crossed his arms and ankles. Deceptively harmless.

"I've heard from your director, and we'll cooperate with you. But you won't get in the way of my mission, understood? Because if you do, your ass is mine, and not in a pleasant way."

"Yes, sir," Ace said.

Ivy didn't speak.

"Agent McGill?" the colonel said, his voice as calm and cool as it could be. Inside, she seethed. But she couldn't let him know that.

"Without us, you wouldn't know the first thing about this sub, Colonel," she said coolly. "Without us, I don't believe you'd even have a mission—but no, I won't get in the way."

Her heart thumped as she met the colonel's gaze. He didn't say anything, merely studied her for a long minute.

"I like passion in a special operator," he said. "The job *should* be personal sometimes, though you always need to strive to stay objective about it. I'll accept your irritation at having this case taken away from you, Agent McGill—but I won't tolerate insubordination. You've had your say. Now I expect you to follow orders if you're going to remain here. Is that clear?"

He hadn't moved a muscle, and yet she felt as if she'd been flayed alive with a very sharp knife. And since she'd never heard of HOT before about an hour ago, she knew this man was in a position of far greater power than her job was worth. A word to the director, perhaps, and she could find herself bounced to the curb. She suddenly got the impression she was here because he'd allowed it and not because of anything Leslie had done.

"Yes, sir."

"Excellent." He pushed away from the desk. "Now come and meet the team, and we'll get you both up to speed with what the plan is."

Ace shot her a look as they followed the colonel from his office. His eyes widened for a second, and his expression said he wasn't precisely thrilled with her. She gave him a hard look in return.

Dammit, she knew she shouldn't mouth off, but she'd worked hard—*they'd* worked hard—to crack this case, and now the military was taking over. She didn't have to like it even if she did have to respect it.

The colonel walked down a corridor and threw a door open. She heard the scrape of boots as probably a dozen people shot to their feet. It reminded her of the one time she'd met her father-in-law. *Ex-father-in-law.* He'd come to Dane's graduation with an entourage that had practically bowed and scraped its way over the campus.

She'd never been fond of the military—and that experience hadn't changed her opinion, that's for sure.

"At ease," Colonel Mendez said.

Ivy kept her chin up as she walked into the room. The men ranged around a table with laptops and papers in front of them. On the screen was a snapshot of the sub and a rundown of the specs.

But it was the man standing beside the screen that caught her attention. Tall, dark blond hair, handsome. Familiar. Too familiar.

Ivy's gut clenched and her heart pounded as she glanced wildly around the room. She felt hot and cold as panic spread through her belly, her bones. She told herself to breathe, not to pass out in front of these men.

This was the goddamn Army. These men were in the *Army*. She could not be standing here looking at her ex-husband, because Dane was in the Navy.

But it *was* him. Even with her eyes closed, she would know it. Bitterness rolled through her like a shockwave. He'd chosen the Navy over her, just like her father had chosen the Navy over her and her mother. She could still feel the shock of Dane announcing he wanted to be a SEAL. And her reaction. God...

Dane stared back at her with cold eyes, and a shiver washed over her. Of course he blamed her. She met his gaze evenly. She wouldn't back down from that look. Not now. Not ever.

Even if her heart did ache with memories of what they'd once been.

FOUR

DANE COULD ONLY STARE AT the front of the room and the woman who'd walked in behind the colonel.

He wanted to blink and make the apparition go away, but it didn't work that way. Ivy was no apparition. She was a flesh and blood woman with long dark hair and curves he'd once worshipped with his mouth and hands. Curves he'd been unable to get enough of at one time.

He remembered hot, dark, sweaty nights between the sheets with her. He remembered thinking she was the center of his universe, and then he remembered the pain that had sliced through him when he'd found out he wasn't the center of hers.

She stared back at him coolly—and then she looked away. He stiffened, but only for a moment.

Fuck her. Fuck her and the horse she rode in on. She didn't mean a damn thing to him anymore, and he wasn't going to let old memories make him nostalgic.

Colonel Mendez was busy introducing the two agents, telling the team that Ivy and—was it Ace?—would be joining them to observe the mission. Dane cut his gaze to Ace, and a slow burn of something flared in the pit of his stomach.

Something he didn't have a right to feel, but it burned through him nevertheless.

The guy was good-looking, muscular, though not as tall as Dane. Was he Ivy's lover as well as her partner? Was he the one getting her kisses and hearing her moans of pleasure? Did he know that's all it would ever be, that she'd never want the same things from him that he wanted from her?

Would she marry him in a drunken haze one night in Vegas and then abandon him a few months later because she didn't want to be with him badly enough to make compromises?

With Ivy, anything was possible. She had an air about her of sweet vulnerability, and yet she was probably one of the toughest women he'd ever known. She'd melted in bed and been fierce outside it. He'd found that addictive at one time.

No more. The kind of women he dated now, when he dated, didn't fascinate him the way Ivy once had. Hell, if he didn't like sex so much, he'd have probably sworn off women altogether after Ivy.

"Have a seat, agents, and my guys will bring you up to date," Colonel Mendez said before he turned and walked out of the room.

Ivy and Ace came over and sat in a couple of empty chairs. Naturally, the chair Ivy chose was right next to the one Dane had been sitting in. Karma was a bitch that way.

"We'll run the briefing again," Matt said. "Everyone take a seat."

Dane hoped someone else would sit in the chair he'd

been occupying, but of course everyone returned to the one they'd been in. Dane walked over and sat down beside Ivy. He heard her intake of breath, and he worked hard not to turn and glare at her.

Four and a half years since they'd called it quits, and she still had the ability to make him angry. And all she'd done was walk into the room.

He could smell her. The shampoo was the same, or maybe it was simply her own scent. She'd always smelled sweet to him, like flowers and candy. He used to love to pull her close and put his nose against her hair when they were out somewhere. Even better, he'd loved stripping her naked and tasting how sweet she was with his lips and tongue.

Someone flipped off the lights, and the presentation ran on the whiteboard. Dane didn't pay a bit of attention because he'd already seen it. He pushed his chair back enough that he was slightly behind Ivy instead of beside her. That's when he dared to glance at her.

She was watching the slides, but her hands were clasped tightly together in her lap. Her knuckles were white. He liked that because it meant she was as rattled by his presence as he'd been with hers.

Or maybe she was angry that she'd been caught unaware like this. Because he had no doubt she hadn't expected him. God knows *what* she'd expected, but he hadn't been it.

Her lids dropped, and then she cut her eyes toward him. Maybe she didn't expect him to be looking at her, or maybe she did. He didn't know, but he didn't look away. Instead, he gave her a slow grin.

And then he winked.

Ivy's heart kicked hard. My God, could it get any worse? Dane was here in the same room. Worse, he was beside her, so damn close, and he grinned as if she were a fresh conquest instead of old news.

She remembered that grin. Remembered when they'd first met in a bar off campus and he'd flashed that grin at her. She'd been unable to speak for a long minute. One of her girlfriends had bumped her side and laughed about it.

But then Dane had strode over, all gorgeous and vibrant, and held out his hand. The band had been playing a slow song, and though she didn't usually dance because she felt too self-conscious, she'd put her hand in his and let him tug her onto the floor. He'd pulled her in close, but not too close.

His touch had been a revelation to her. She'd burned where his hands rested on her waist, and she'd tilted her face up to look at him.

He'd grinned again. "I'm Dane."

"Ivy."

He'd run those hands up her sides, back down. Never touching her inappropriately but setting her on fire anyway.

"Well, Ivy, I think this is going to be the beginning of something special…"

And it had been. For five months, until they'd gone to Vegas and gotten married on impulse, and for three months after that, until their relationship began to fracture over the future. Over *choices.*

Ivy gave her head a tiny shake and concentrated on the slides. She knew most of the information already because she'd been the one to uncover it when she'd interviewed the worker they'd found alive at the jungle shipyard. The Ruizes had been dealing with a Middle Eastern terror group. She didn't doubt that they'd planned on fleecing the terrorists instead of selling them a sub, because that was how they operated, but clearly they hadn't anticipated the buyers showing up with an assault team.

Another slide flashed up on the screen, this one of a missile. The guy who'd been speaking paused here and gave her and Ace a hard look.

"This is why we're involved now, in case you were wondering."

"We know there's a terror group involved," Ace said. "And that they were planning on detonating a dirty bomb on the Eastern Seaboard."

"That's not a bomb," Ivy said, studying the missile. The markings were Cyrillic.

"No, it's not," Dane chimed in beside her. "It's a Russian-made missile, designed to deliver a nuclear warhead from a bomber. It's compact enough to fit into this sub."

She didn't want to look at him, but to ignore him in front of these men would be strange. Clearly, no one in this room had any idea that she and Dane had once been married. She didn't plan to tell them either. There were already enough complications here. She didn't need another one.

She swiveled her head to meet his gaze head-on. It was as if she'd driven her car into an embankment. That's how suddenly and how strongly his presence impacted her.

"Thank you..." She let her gaze drop to his name tag as if she didn't know who he was. "...Lieutenant Erikson."

"Anytime, doll."

And there was that megawatt grin again. Beside her, she could feel Ace stiffen. He was a good partner, and he took slights to her as personally as he did those to himself.

Someone cleared his throat. The captain in charge of the briefing continued, filling them in until they reached the end and someone flipped the lights back on.

Ivy knew better than to look at Dane again. But she could feel him looking at her. Boring a hole through her.

"Hey, you got a problem, man?"

It was Ace coming to the rescue precisely when she didn't need him to do a damn thing. Ivy whipped around to glare at her partner. "It's fine, Ace."

Ace looked militant. "It's not fine. You're as qualified to be here as anyone, and this guy"—he waved a hand in Dane's general direction—"keeps staring at you like he's at happy hour looking for a hookup instead of in a room full of equals. Care to explain that, asshole?"

Ivy winced as Dane unfolded himself and got to his feet. All six foot four inches of him. Ace stood as well. Ace was considerably shorter, but Ivy knew from experience he wasn't going to let that intimidate him.

Ivy shot to her feet and put a hand on Ace's arm. Dane's gaze lasered in on her hand, then back up to her face.

"Do you want to explain it, Ivy? Or do you want me to?" Dane asked. So polite, as if they were at tea instead of inside a war room.

"Explain what?" Ace demanded. "That you're an asshole?"

If Ivy could have glared a hole into Dane, she would have. But of course he wasn't content to leave the past in the past. He wasn't going to act like she was simply another professional he had to deal with. He was going to drag up the whole thing right here for everyone's amusement.

Dane didn't do subtle. She knew that from experience.

Ivy met his stare with a hard look of her own. "Since you're having so much fun, you go right on ahead."

Dane let that slow grin spread over his face again. He looked like he was having a good time, but she knew looks were deceiving. She knew he was angry and lashing out because he still blamed her for the breakdown in their marriage.

"Well, Ace," Dane drawled, "I guess Ivy didn't tell you about me, and that kinda hurts. But the truth is, Ivy and I already know each other *really* well. So well that we decided we couldn't live together anymore—isn't that right, baby?"

"Aw, fuck me," Ace said, turning to look at her. "Is this the ex-husband? Really?"

Ivy gritted her teeth. "The one and only. See what a charmer he is?"

FIVE

"IS THIS GOING TO BE a problem?"

Colonel Mendez sat behind his desk and frowned at her and Dane. After their revelation in the briefing room, one of the guys sighed heavily and said, "I'll take them to see the colonel."

Ivy might have argued that point, but Dane walked out on the man's heels, and Ivy decided she'd better follow or get left out of the conversation. And since she was pretty sure Colonel Mendez had the power to cut her out of this mission, she wasn't letting Dane speak for her because she already knew what his opinion of her presence would be.

"Not for me," Ivy said even as her pulse thrummed and heat rolled beneath her skin.

"No, sir," Dane said, all military rigidity and properness now. "I was surprised. I imagine Ivy was surprised as well."

"Didn't part on the best of terms, I take it?" Mendez arched an eyebrow.

"We haven't spoken in over four years," Ivy offered.

"I imagine that's due more to our jobs than malice. I have no feelings one way or the other about Lieutenant Erikson. Our marriage is in the past. For all I know, he's remarried."

"Nope," Dane said. "Not on your life. Once was enough."

Mendez's other eyebrow went up. "Do I need to repeat the question, Lieutenant?"

"No, sir. It won't be a problem. Lost my head for a second, sir."

Mendez glared at them both for good measure. "That's mighty good to know. Because if it *is* a problem, for either one of you, I'm removing you both from this mission. Is that clear?"

Ivy's face burned hotter. No way in hell was she letting Dane get her kicked off this mission. Not when she had a personal stake in seeing the sub captured. The Ruizes had killed her mother and many more poor and desperate people like her—and Ivy wasn't letting that happen anymore. Not if she could help it. Capturing the sub was only part of the equation. There was still so much to do in order to dismantle the Ruiz network, but she'd start with the submarine and their ability to make more of them.

And then there was the fact that if she got sent home from this mission maybe her bosses would lose faith in her ability to handle the job. Maybe she'd get shuffled off to something besides the Ruiz case.

She couldn't allow that. She'd spent too many years trying to run the Ruizes to ground, and she wasn't about to have that taken away from her now. Especially not by a man she'd left in the past.

"Understood," she said.

"Yes, sir," Dane replied.

The colonel waved a hand. "Good. Now get the fuck out of my office and get back to work."

Dane shortened his steps as they walked back to the briefing room. Ivy walked beside him, her chin in the air, her long dark hair falling in a luxurious silken wave down her back. She wore a black pantsuit with a red blouse and what his mom would call sensible heels. He knew for a fact Ivy looked fantastic in short skirts and high heels, but clearly she opted for something a little more sedate while working.

Except the shirt was low enough to give a tantalizing glimpse of cleavage, and since Dane knew what those breasts looked like bare, he couldn't help but let his gaze stray there a bit more often than it should.

Ivy stopped suddenly and Dane was caught short. He turned to face her. She'd put her hands on her hips and her face was flushed.

Still so fucking pretty.

"I can't believe you did that," she said. "What in the hell were you thinking?"

Dane dragged his gaze from the scoop neck of her top. "Why are you wearing clothes that hide your figure?"

Ivy blinked. And then her face grew redder. "Un-fucking-believable! I'm being serious here, and you're talking to me about my *clothes?* What about your clothes, asshole? Why are you wearing camouflage?"

"It's my uniform."

Ivy poked him in the chest with a manicured finger-nail. "Exactly, dickhead. We aren't dressing for a night out on the town here, are we? Not to mention your right to discuss my wardrobe ended when you walked out on me."

A hot ball of anger coiled tight in Dane's chest. He worked real hard not to let it explode. "When I walked out on you? Honey, you told me to get out, if I remember rightly. Told me to go join the fucking SEALs and stay out of your life."

"You were going to join anyway. You told me that. I told you not to come back if you did."

He couldn't help the sarcasm in his tone. "Same as I told you when you wanted to join the DEA, right?"

She had the grace to look ashamed—for about half a second. "That was different, and you know it. You knew why."

Yes, he knew that her mother had died from an acci-dental drug overdose after her father abandoned them and that Ivy had spent a few years in foster care before going to live with her grandmother. He also knew that she'd had a passion to prevent drugs from reaching the streets. It was her calling, and he couldn't argue with that. But the Navy had been his calling, and she hadn't understood. Neither had his parents. His father had gone particularly ballistic at the announcement. It had felt as if everyone in his life who was supposed to support him had bailed on him.

Which they had.

"And before you go getting all self-righteous," she continued, "you weren't precisely happy about it."

"No, but I was supportive. Because you wanted it, Ivy. Because I loved you."

And when you loved someone, you supported them.

He didn't miss the way her green eyes darkened for a second or the way even saying those words formed a lump in his throat. Yeah, he'd loved her. He'd learned the hard way that it wasn't a good idea. Thanks to Ivy, he wasn't ever letting himself get so emotionally involved with a woman again.

He'd had no idea what love was supposed to be, but he'd thought it meant you did whatever it took to make the other person happy. Yeah, he'd been an idiot all right. Never again.

"If I'd never joined the DEA, if I'd followed you around the world, sat in port and waited for months while you were gone, you'd have been perfectly happy to let that happen. I needed more, Dane."

"You knew when you met me what my plans were," he growled. "If you didn't like it, then why the fuck did you stay? Why did you marry me?"

She'd been the first person he'd told that he planned to join the Navy rather than the Army as expected. He hadn't told her about the SEALs at that point because he hadn't realized it himself.

She closed her eyes for a second. "It never changes, does it? We've had this argument before. Clearly, we don't understand each other. We never did. And we shouldn't have gotten married. It was wrong."

"Didn't feel like that at the time."

She snorted softly. "You know it's true though. We were young and dumb and hot for each other. That's not enough to build a life together."

Dane shook his head. "There are worse things than being hot for each other. It's a start."

She pinched the bridge of her nose. "I can't do this right now. We sat there and told that man this wasn't going to be a problem. And I really need it not to be because I have work to do. I want to find these motherfuckers and get that sub, and then I want to go back to nailing the Ruizes to the wall."

Dane put his hands up in surrender. "Not a problem, sweetheart. I'm not the one who started it this time. You did."

"And you never answered the question. Why did you have to tell everyone I was your ex like that?"

"You think they don't have a right to know? When they have to put their asses on the line in order to find these terrorists before they destroy innocent lives?"

"But what does that have to do with us?"

"If I have to give you an order, will you do what you're told or tell me to fuck off?"

She bristled. "Who said you'd be giving me orders? I'm not a military operative, Dane."

"No, but you're assigned to this operation. What if I'm the one giving you the order? You think they don't have a right to know there's a problem between us when lives depend on the answer?"

She crossed her arms. All it served to do was lift her breasts higher. Dane gritted his teeth and kept his eyes on her face.

"Maybe so, but we could have gone to see the colonel privately. Or you could have announced I was your ex-wife. No need for all the drama and male posturing."

It was Dane's turn to snort. She really didn't get it. He started down the hall, then called back to her, "Yeah, but where's the fun in that?"

SIX

IVY WAS GOING TO GO crazy before this mission was over. She got out of her car and locked it, then headed into her apartment building, her mind full of Dane Erikson and HOT, her hands full of groceries.

It had been a long day. Not only because of Dane, but also because of the potential for catastrophe. They had to find that submarine, and they had to put a stop to the terrorists who were planning to sail a nuke into some unsuspecting harbor.

Based on the time the sub could operate underwater and how secure the terrorists potentially were in their plan, the nuke could end up anywhere. Miami, Virginia Beach, Baltimore, Boston—or maybe Los Angeles or San Diego.

Yeah, the damn thing could be anywhere, though it seemed most likely the East Coast was the target since the sub had last been seen in Cartagena. The US Navy was on high alert, as were the Coast Guard and the port authorities. But the ocean was mighty big, and the sub mighty small. Talk about your basic needle in a haystack.

Ivy juggled her groceries and unlocked the door. This

was new territory for her, but she understood the urgency—who wouldn't? You'd have to be insane not to get why this was important.

Still didn't mean she liked the idea of working with Dane. Maybe she should have called Leslie up and told her she couldn't do it after all—but that wasn't the way Ivy operated. She was stronger than that.

Dane was a complication, but she could handle him. Even if seeing him again made her heart ache and her body light up in ways she really didn't appreciate.

Damn his handsome face and spectacular body anyway.

She set her groceries on the counter, then took everything out of the bags and put it away. The light on her answering machine blinked incessantly, so she went over and pressed the button. She knew a lot of people only used their cell phones, but she kept a landline too. In the event of a catastrophe, cell towers wouldn't work while landlines still could.

Ivy frowned at the thought. She'd always been paranoid. Always planning for the worst that could happen rather than the best. She'd planned her entire life that way. Dane used to tease her about that.

Ow. She rubbed in the vicinity of her heart and deleted the first message, a generic spiel from a telemarketer offering to cut her credit card interest rates in half. The second was dead air. The third started to play...

We know who you are, Ivy McGill... we know where to find you...

The message ended with a sharp beep, and Ivy's heart kicked inside her chest. She was accustomed to being threatened, but this was the first time anyone had ever phoned her at home.

And her number wasn't simply unlisted—it was un-published. Unavailable to anyone except those people she wanted to have it—other than random telemarketers who targeted every known number regardless of who lived there, of course.

Out of instinct, Ivy pulled her gun and swept through her apartment. There'd been no signs of forced entry, but that didn't mean anything these days. Criminals were clev-er. Drug dealers like the Ruizes were even more so.

She didn't find anything that indicated anyone had been inside, and the apartment was clean. But she had to take the threat, however vague, seriously. She wasn't go-ing to stop working and go into hiding, because that would mean the criminals had won—but she would go to a hotel while her agency sorted this out.

She went and grabbed her bugout bag and her com-puter, then headed back out again. She phoned Ace once she was in the car and told him what had happened.

"Ivy, what the fuck? Do you think it's the Ruizes?"

"Who else could it be? We've been working on bring-ing them down for months now."

Months in which she'd traveled a lot, slept a little, and eaten a load of fast-food crap as they stalked the Ruiz-es and waited for a break. They'd thought they'd had it with the submarines. And then the fucking Freedom Force had to get involved.

Ace snorted. "Yeah, true. But what if it's someone fucking with you? What about that musclehead you call an ex-husband? Would he do something like this to screw with you?"

Ivy's gut clenched. "What? No way! Dane might still

be pissed off at me, but he wouldn't threaten me. Not even as a joke."

"Okay, okay, calm down. If you say so, I believe you. Where you headed?"

"I'm checking into a hotel near the base. Might as well stay near HOT HQ since we'll be working there for the foreseeable future."

"Yeah, sounds good. You calling Leslie next?"

Ivy bit her lower lip. There was the possibility Leslie would pull her from the HOT mission over this—but the threat was real, and Ivy wasn't stupid. Leslie had to be informed.

"Yes, I'm telling her. She can get a trace put on that call, see if we find anything."

Ace blew out a breath. "Yeah, good plan... You need anything, Ivy? Need me to come watch your back to-night?"

"No, I'm good. I'll see you in the morning. It was a vague threat, Ace. We've certainly heard worse."

"True dat. Let me know where you're staying."

"I will."

They finished the call and then Ivy phoned Leslie. Her boss wasn't precisely happy, but she said she'd start the IT forensics department working on the call. If they figured out where it came from—where it really came from and not just the VOIP masking system the caller had used to hide the number from her caller ID—maybe they'd learn something useful.

Until then, there was nothing Ivy could do except check into the hotel and keep doing her job.

After she was settled, she texted Ace her information and then opened up her computer and started searching through some of the unclassified files she had on the Ruiz-es. There was a lot to think about with the missing sub and the Freedom Force, but the Ruizes were her specialty. And maybe something in the files would trigger a thought about the terrorists.

Ivy had been scanning the files for approximately ten minutes when there was a hard knock on her door. Her heart leapt, and she shoved the computer aside to reach for her gun.

"Ivy! Open up! It's Dane."

Ivy blinked. Dane? Here? Oh, holy shit.

She went to the door and opened it, though she didn't slide the chain back. Dane loomed on the other side, his face thunderous. He was dressed in jeans and a navy T-shirt that molded the hard planes of his sculpted chest like a second skin.

She swallowed. "What are you doing here?"

"Heard you'd moved in. I'm down the hall."

Ivy couldn't believe what she was hearing. "Wait... you're staying in this hotel?"

"I'm TDY, Ivy. I don't live in DC. Yeah, I'm staying here. Now open up."

She clung to the door like it was a lifeline. "Well thanks for checking in, but I'm fine. Now go away."

He pushed his foot in the door when she would have shut it. "Mendez said someone threatened you."

Ivy stopped trying to push the door closed. "Why would he tell you that?"

"Because we're on the same team. He told everyone."

"Jesus, you military types and your need for disclo-sure." She'd known Colonel Mendez, as the HOT com-mander, would need to be informed of her new location.

She hadn't known he'd be told everything—or that he'd share it with the whole damn team. "This is irrelevant to the current mission."

"No threat is irrelevant to the mission, baby."

"Don't call me baby."

She thought he might have growled. "You used to love when I called you baby."

"Used to. Past tense."

"For fuck's sake, Ivy, let me in."

"Get your foot out of the door and I will."

His eyes narrowed. "If you don't, I'll break the fucking thing down. Got it?"

She was tempted to shut the door and leave it that way. She had no doubt Dane would follow through on his threat—and then the police would come and haul him away for damaging hotel property. Probably wouldn't look so good on his military reports, come to think of it.

Not that she cared. She totally did not care.

Still, she slid the chain off the latch and opened the door.

SEVEN

DANE WAS EVEN MORE IMPOSING in full view than the slice of him she'd had earlier. God, had she really lain beneath that powerful body and felt it moving inside hers? Had she worshipped his body with her hands and mouth and thought she'd found nirvana?

She turned away and moved back to the couch in the living area of the suite. Damn, she should have gone to a regular hotel instead of the kind of temporary living suites that government workers and business travelers frequented for long stints away from home. But she'd gone where she was most familiar, so the fact the place was probably chock-full of military on TDY assignments or government contractors going to classes on the base really shouldn't surprise her.

Dane came inside and locked the door behind him. Then he stood there and shoved his hands into his pockets. He still looked angry as she sat down and leaned back to watch him. She was doing her damnedest to act unaffected, but she could feel her pulse thrumming like a hummingbird's wings in her throat.

"So why did you want to come in? Didn't have enough fun on memory lane earlier?"

Dane tugged a chair from the table and turned it around, sitting down backward, his legs straddling the back, his arms lying casually over the top.

"We were married for six months, Ivy. Together for almost a year. I care that someone threatened you."

Ivy blinked. Tears wanted to spring up behind her eyes, but she wasn't going to let them. That would be too much. There was too much water under the bridge for her to get emotional now.

"I don't need you to care."

And it was true. She'd been through a lot over the past four and a half years, and Dane hadn't been there for any of it. She'd been threatened. Shot at. Held hostage once. Where was he then?

"You don't get to decide that."

Ivy turned her head and stared at nothing. Then she rubbed a hand over her eyes. Damn, she was tired. "We haven't spoken in over four years. I find your presence here very disconcerting."

He sighed. "You aren't alone in that, Ivy. But we're here... together... working on the same mission. I can't act like I'm not concerned."

She really wanted to throw something. "You didn't have a problem being unconcerned for four years. I don't see why that needs to change now."

He shot to his feet and paced over to the window and then back again. He reminded her of a caged animal, angry and ready to pounce. If she let him, he would tear her throat out.

"What did you expect me to do? Call you up from

time to time and ask how you were?"

She swallowed. "No, of course not."

But maybe it would have been nice to hear from him every once in a while. When he'd walked out of her life, she'd waited for him to walk back into it. Waited for him to cool down and come home.

He hadn't, and she hadn't gone after him. They'd both been too proud to give an inch of ground. It had seemed like such a small thing, in a way, at first—and then it just kept getting bigger and bigger until they reached the point of no return.

He stopped and put his hands on his hips, staring down at her angrily. "And no way in hell were you calling me either, right?"

She looked down at her hands lying in her lap. "What would have been the point, Dane? You made it clear how you felt. Talking only ended up in arguing. Neither one of us enjoyed that."

"You know, when I went on my first mission as a SEAL, I kept hoping I'd come back and find a message from you. I think I must have still thought there was a chance. But when I got back, there was nothing. That's when I knew it was really over for good."

Ivy swallowed the hard knot in her throat. "I didn't even know you were gone."

"Yeah, but what does that matter? You could have left a message on my phone because you missed me. You didn't."

Oh, but she had missed him. Terribly. Every minute of every day since he'd walked out on her. But she didn't know how to breach the divide. Didn't know how to give them what they both wanted and make it all work.

So she'd thrown herself into work and tried to ignore the fact that her heart had shattered into a million pieces. She'd needed to be strong, needed to take care of herself. She knew what happened when a woman let herself believe a man would be there for her.

She hadn't thought Dane was anything like her father, but then he'd gotten angry and walked out, and she'd known right then that every man was only a heartbeat away from abandoning you. Even if she hadn't had her parents as proof, Granny had told her so more than once— Grandpa had left her with three sons to feed. Just up and walked out one day. The end.

When a man got tired of dealing, they left. She knew it to her core, and she wasn't ever letting herself be that vulnerable again.

Ivy got to her feet. "Look, I appreciate your concern, but I'm fine. You know where I am now, and you can comfort yourself with the knowledge I'm not leaving this room again until morning if it makes you feel better."

Dane stared at her for a long minute. And then he shook his head and laughed. The sound wasn't humorous though.

"Jesus, Ivy. You're the best in the world at avoiding the shit you don't want to talk about. I don't know why I thought anything had changed in the past few years." He stalked past her and then stopped at the door with his hand on the chain. "I'm in 224, two rooms down on the left. Call if you need anything. I *will* have your back. Even if you'd prefer I didn't."

Ivy didn't sleep too well, but she was up early and back at HOT before seven a.m. She didn't see Dane at the hotel again, but the minute she walked inside HOT HQ, he was there, looking much too appealing in his cammies. He held a go-cup of coffee in one hand and stood with two other guys. His gaze slid over to her.

She gritted her teeth and kept her chin up. These guys all knew that she and Dane had been married. In a way, it was kind of a relief. That thought made her pause for a second—huh, maybe he'd been right after all. Now that everyone knew, there was nothing to hide, nothing to feel guilty for. It was all about the work now. Even if being in the same room with Dane again made her heart pound a little bit harder and her brain insist on conjuring up images of him without his clothes.

Colonel Mendez arrived a few minutes later, and everyone snapped to attention. Even Ace. Ivy simply stood straight and still and waited until the colonel told everyone to be at ease. Then she sank into a chair and sipped her coffee.

"We've had intel that indicates our target might be headed for Miami. The Navy is sweeping the waters around Cuba and trying to intercept."

Ivy thought that might be an end to it then. She and Ace would be sent back to the DEA and the Navy would find the sub.

"Agent McGill," the colonel said, and Ivy's head

snapped up.

"Yes?"

"How do you feel about going to the Keys?"

"The Keys, sir?"

"Yes."

"I don't think I understand."

"Miami's too logical a guess for where they're head-ed," one of the men said. The name tape on his chest said Gordon. What everyone called him was Flash. "They know it as well as we do. And that's not how the Freedom Force operates. They won't sail into a port—*any* port."

"No," the colonel said. "They'll put into the Keys somewhere, meet up with the sleeper cell that's currently there, and truck the missile overland—but not to Miami."

"Where are they going then?" Ace asked. He looked all kinds of fascinated right about now. Ivy was too, but damned if she'd show it.

The colonel pointed at the map of Florida on-screen. "Tampa. US Central Command is based at MacDill Air Force Base, as well as Special Operations Command and Command Central. It's a helluva target."

Ivy shuddered. It was indeed. Wipe out CENTCOM and you dealt a severe blow to the US's ability to fight wars in the Middle East—not to mention the hit to the na-tion's morale should such a thing happen.

"But wouldn't it be easier to sail into port in Tampa?" Ivy asked. "Why risk trying to offload it in the Keys?"

"It would be easier," Dane said, "but these guys aren't exactly experienced seamen. It takes a special kind of person to be a submariner, and I'm going to guess these men aren't it. They'll be claustrophobic and half-crazy by the time they reach the Keys—assuming the Navy doesn't pick them up first."

"That's right," the colonel said. "And if the Navy doesn't get them first, we can't let that nuke into the US. We're intercepting it in the Keys."

"And if we can't find them?" Ivy asked.

The colonel's dark eyes didn't waver. "You'd better hope we do, Agent McGill. The alternative is that tens of thousands of people die—and Florida becomes a nuclear wasteland."

EIGHT

DC WAS MUGGY, BUT FLORIDA was muggier. Ivy twisted her hair up onto her head and secured it with a ponytail holder from her purse. Then she grabbed her suitcase handle again and kept walking down the trail.

They weren't in Key West itself but on a smaller island called Emerald Key. It was still popular, but not as jam-packed with tourists as Key West. The team was staying in a resort that featured small bungalows tucked away among the palms. Ivy had her own bungalow thankfully. The beaches weren't far, and there were several restaurants and shops on the main street. It was on Emerald Key that the Freedom Force sleeper cell was supposedly located.

One of the men ran a small marina while the others worked in the various restaurants and businesses on the island. They had dossiers on the men from the CIA, and the plan was to track each of them down and follow them as they went about their daily business. If HOT was lucky—and they really needed to be lucky, Ivy thought— they'd find the submarine and the nuclear weapon before it could do any damage.

Ivy stuck the key in the lock and opened the door. Blessedly cool air hit her as she walked inside. The bungalow wasn't big—a main living area, a kitchenette, and a bedroom with an en suite bath—but it was clean and cool.

And it was all hers. There were definitely some perks to being the only woman on a mission. As she understood it, there were a couple of women who worked for HOT as special operators—but they were on other assignments at the moment. That was fine with her because she preferred to be alone. Ivy kicked off her shoes and unzipped her case. Ace had escorted her back to her apartment to grab some clothes for this trip. The IT department was still working on a trace on her mysterious phone call, but there'd been nothing further.

Ivy pulled out a long sundress with spaghetti straps and some clean underwear. There was time for a shower before she had to meet with the guys, so she went into the bathroom and turned on the water. She set her clothes on the counter and her gun on a high shelf inside the shower enclosure, away from the spray. Once the water was hot, she stepped under the stream and sighed. It had been a long day, and she needed the relaxation a good hot shower could provide.

You need more than a shower for relaxation. You need a big cock and a man who knows how to use it.

Ivy shoved that thought away. Hard. But Dane was in her head now, and no amount of wishing him away would make him go. She closed her eyes and let herself picture his body—smooth muscle, bronzed skin, a happy trail of dark gold hair arrowing down from his belly to his cock. And then, yes, that beautiful hard cock of his, rising straight and proud and ready to take her to heaven.

Ivy bit her lip on a moan. Her nipples peaked and her pussy ached. Against her better judgment, she slipped a finger between her folds, found the slick bundle of nerves at the center. Lightning sizzled along her nerve endings as she stroked her clit.

How long had it been since she'd come? It felt like months, though it couldn't really be that long.

Though maybe it could.

Ivy stroked herself, her body tightening and aching from being so long denied. It wouldn't take much at all—

A sound made her eyes snap open—and a man stood inside the bathroom, the open door silhouetting his dark form. For half a second, she thought it might be Dane.

But he took a step toward her and she realized he was too dark, too short to be Dane. Ivy's heart froze—and then she reached for her weapon.

Dane was surveying the property around his dwelling when he heard the sharp crack of a gunshot coming from the direction of Ivy's bungalow. He sprang into motion, crossing the short distance between bungalows and leaping up the steps. The door was locked. He shoved his shoulder into it a couple of times, but the chain held. Drawing his .45, he skirted the small bungalow and went around to the back entrance.

The door was open. After clearing the entry, he leapt into the room, ready to do battle. There was no one inside, no signs of a struggle.

"Ivy!" he shouted.

"Dane?"

He followed the sound of her voice and ended up in the bathroom. The steam from the shower thickened the air, and he went over and turned it off. Ivy leaned against the wall, her gun hanging limply in her hand.

She was naked, and his body stirred at the sight of her creamy skin and wet hair. Dane tamped down on his libido and reached over to take the gun from her. She looked up then, her green eyes a little stunned.

"What happened?" he demanded.

She swallowed. "I was in the shower when I opened my eyes and saw a man standing inside the door. I grabbed my gun from the shelf—I fired, but my hands were wet and my aim slipped."

Dane reached for a towel and handed it to her, then turned and went out the door so he could sweep the bungalow again. There was no one inside and no one lurking in the bushes. Whoever had broken in was gone now. He could try to follow them, but in the end he couldn't leave Ivy. Dane went back into the bathroom to find Ivy wrapped in the towel and combing her hair with deliberate strokes.

When she'd told him she wanted to join the DEA, he'd hoped like hell she wanted to be an analyst, someone who studied the intel and made reports. He'd never pictured her in the field, but of course that's where she wanted to be.

And he hadn't been there for most of it. Hadn't actively seen her in danger before now.

He didn't fucking like it. He holstered his gun and

stood there waiting for her to say something.

"I shouldn't have missed," she said angrily.

"It could happen to anyone," he told her. "Your hands were wet and you were startled."

Her eyes met his in the mirror. She was pissed. "*You* wouldn't miss. You're trained to do nearly everything while soaking wet, I imagine."

"Yes." He said it simply because it was true. As a SEAL, he was expected to spend a lot of time in the water. He was as comfortable there as he was anywhere. "But you aren't a SEAL, Ivy."

She sniffed. "Did you find where he broke in?"

"The back door's open, but it doesn't look forced. Did you check it when you came inside?"

He could see the color creeping into her face. "No. I had a lot on my mind and I… didn't."

He knew that admission galled her. Ivy was proud and—usually—thorough. In school, she'd been the one who wrote her papers weeks before they were due while he was usually floundering on the last day.

"You can't stay here. It's not safe."

Ivy spun to face him. "And what do you propose I do? Go home? Not happening, mister."

"That's not what I said," he grated, his voice rough. "You need to move bungalows. And you shouldn't be alone."

Her mouth fell open a little. "In spite of what just happened, I *can* take care of myself. I was caught off guard this time, but it won't happen again. No resort Peeping Tom is going to scare me a second time."

Dane wanted to grab her and shake her. "And what if it wasn't a Peeping Tom? What if this is related to that threat you got back in DC?"

Ivy blinked. "How could it be? Unless someone is following me everywhere, or they've tapped my phone—which they have *not*, by the way—how could it be related? And why? It's not like I've discovered the holy grail to taking down the Ruizes and they need to stop me. I'm a thorn in their side, but no deeper or more annoying than I've ever been."

He knew that had to pain her to admit. Fighting drugs was often like playing Whac-A-Mole. Stop one conduit and others sprang up in their place. Ivy, being the meticulous sort, wouldn't like that one bit.

"You can't ignore the possibility. You need to move. And you need backup."

Before he could say anything more, voices he recognized came from inside the bungalow. He gave Ivy a hard look and then left her alone so she could get dressed. Some of his new teammates clustered in the living area, weapons drawn, while others still came in from the rear door.

"It's okay, guys," Dane said. "The area is clear."

Ace shot toward him, looking about as pissed off as a fighting rooster. "Where's Ivy?" he demanded. "And what the fuck happened here?"

Dane resisted the urge to wrap his hands around the little fucker's throat, but only barely. He didn't like the guy, no matter that he seemed to care about Ivy's welfare. Probably because he had what Dane didn't, which was a relationship with Ivy that wasn't combative. He got to be with her and see her smile, hear her laugh. Dane hadn't heard her laugh in years.

And he damn sure hadn't been the recipient of one of her smiles in ages.

"Ivy's fine. Someone busted in here and startled her while she was showering. No sign of the intruder."

Ace puffed up. "Are you sure it wasn't you, asshole? Trying to get a peep at the ex? Get your jollies for old times' sake?"

Dane growled and took a step toward Ace, but Flash was there, wrapping a hand around Dane's arm and squeezing. He hadn't had a lot of time to get to know these guys, but they'd absorbed his presence like he was one of them. They had his back, and that meant a lot.

"Not helpful," Flash said in a low voice. "Focus on the task at hand."

"Shut the fuck up, Agent Martin," Matt said, "or you can be sent home on the next plane out of here. You're here to observe, not comment, got it?"

Ace grumbled something, but he turned away and went over to flip through the resort flyers sitting on the table. Dane didn't think he was really seeing the brochures so much as he was doing something to keep himself from exploding. But still, Dane hoped the asshole booked a shark cage tour in a faulty cage...

Focus.

"We have to move her," Dane said.

"Agreed," Matt replied. "Big Mac and I will swap with Ivy."

Kev MacDonald nodded in agreement. Someone had told Dane that Kev's wife was part of the team, which he found fucking amazing since women weren't allowed to be SEALs, but she wasn't on this op. She was in DC, working on an intel assignment. Nick Brandon's fiancée was a member too—a fucking sniper of all damn things.

"She can't stay alone." Dane didn't like the idea of

Ivy being by herself, even if she was proficient with a weapon. She was no damn sniper. *You don't really know that, dude.*

Yeah, yeah he did. Otherwise they'd be cleaning up a body instead of wondering who'd broken into her bungalow and where the asshole had gone.

Ace snorted as he turned back to them. "And who's going to stay with her, buddy? You? Like hell."

"No one is staying with me," Ivy ground out.

Everyone turned as she walked out of the bathroom. She was wearing a long, body-hugging black dress and sandals. Every sweet curve was evident, and Dane's throat tightened. Jesus, how could he still be so attracted to this woman?

"I'll change bungalows, but I don't need a babysitter."

"No, you don't need a babysitter—but you do need a bodyguard."

She whipped her head around to glare at Dane. "You don't get to have an opinion about my life anymore, Dane. You gave up that right years ago."

Dane wanted to punch something. "This isn't personal, Ivy. It's fucking common sense. You need someone watching your back."

"And that someone is gonna be me," Ace said, walking over to stand beside Ivy. "She's my partner, and we take care of each other."

Matt's eyes narrowed as he studied them all. "No, it's not you, Ace," he said coolly. "This is my operation and you're an observer. You're staying with Fiddler."

Chase Daniels nodded, his expression brooking no argument. "That's right, man, you're with me."

"Dane, you're with Ivy," Matt said. "Try not to kill each other, you hear?"

"If you want that, then you shouldn't put us together," Ivy snapped.

Matt turned to look at her. "Sorry, Agent McGill, but it makes the most sense. You two know each other, you don't like each other, and there'll be no awkwardness about staying in the same bungalow. You've seen each other naked, and you're both apparently done with that part of the relationship. If I stick one of my other guys with you, who the fuck knows what will happen? I can't afford any distractions—not to mention that Dane might explode if he thought someone else was making moves on you."

"Why the fuck would I care?" Dane asked.

Matt snorted. "Dude, we always care. You might not want the lollipop anymore, but you don't want anyone else having it either."

Ivy's eyes widened. She popped her hands on her hips. "I am *not* a lollipop, and I won't be ordered around like my opinion doesn't matter—"

"But it doesn't, Agent McGill," Matt said. "You're an observer, and you observe at the pleasure of Colonel Mendez—to whom I report. If you don't like what I've told you to do, there's a plane back to DC with a seat for you. Your choice."

If eyes could shoot laser beams, Ivy's would have done so right about then. Dane didn't think he'd ever seen her so pissed, even when she'd been glaring at him and telling him that he could be a SEAL or he could be with her. She'd made him so fucking mad, he'd told her he'd rather be a SEAL than put up with her shit another minute.

56

Yeah, what a great day that had been.

"Fine," Ivy said, drawing herself up to her full five foot four inches. She somehow managed to look down her nose as if she were about six inches taller. It was a helluva trick. "But don't you dare blame me when this turns out to be a bad idea."

"It won't be… will it, Viking?" Matt arched one eyebrow expectantly.

Dane forced himself to smile. He could back out and let someone else guard Ivy… but damn if the Army guy hadn't figured him out after all. He didn't like the idea of someone else staying with her. Didn't trust that another man wouldn't be so blinded by her charms that he might not pay as much attention to her safety as he should.

No, it had to be Dane.

"Not at all," he said. "I'm a professional, and I take my job seriously."

"Excellent," Matt said. "Now let's get moving."

NINE

OH, THIS WAS A BAD idea. No matter what Dane had said, it was bad.

Ivy stood in the living area of the bungalow she now inhabited with her ex-freaking-husband and gazed at the two bedroom doors sitting side by side. They were both open, and Dane was moving around on the other side of one of them. Ivy strode over and peeked in. When she saw which room Dane was in, she took the opposite one.

It didn't take long to hang her clothes and put her toiletries in the bathroom—the *shared* bathroom, for heaven's sake. She thought about closing the bedroom door and locking it for a while so she could lie down and think, but that wouldn't work because how could she think with Dane next door?

Ivy chafed her arms as she returned to the living area. When she'd first seen that man in her bathroom, she'd had a split second of hoping it was Dane. But of course it wasn't—and that was a good thing, really. She didn't need to have sex with her ex-husband, which she would have wanted to do pretty badly if he'd been the one who'd walked in on her in the shower earlier.

Because it had been him she'd pictured while she touched herself. His hands and mouth she remembered. His cock entering her body.

"You doing okay?"

She spun to find Dane watching her. Her heart skipped a beat as she let her eyes slide over his face. Oh, it was so unfair he was that pretty. That damned appealing.

"I'm fine," she said, trying to infuse her voice with starch instead of honey. Because the honey wanted to drip into her tone for some reason, which wasn't appropriate anymore with him.

"Matt sent someone to inquire about the resort staff. It's entirely possible he was there for some maintenance and got distracted when he saw you in the shower."

Ivy snorted. "Yes, he came through the back door, heard the shower, kept on going, and opened the bathroom door when it was clear someone was in there. He was very startled. Probably sucking down a Jack and Coke somewhere and trying to recover."

Dane spread his hands. "Hey, I don't believe it either, but we have to check all the angles. If he was a maintenance man with a penchant for spying on guests, that's better than nothing. It would also mean that whoever threatened you isn't here looking for you."

Ivy frowned. She didn't think the Ruizes had come for her in the Keys because the timing was wrong for that, but what if they had? What if they were crazy enough to make a move now instead of at any other point in the past few years? Maybe they blamed her for their lost submarine, or maybe they thought she'd lead them to it.

Ivy shook her head. That was craziness right there.

"I put nothing past the Ruiz brothers, but even this is a bit too far-fetched for them."

Dane shrugged. Then he went and grabbed a bottle of water from the fridge. When he held out one for her, she took it.

"Whoever it was, they'll have to go through me now," he said, his expression hard.

She knew he meant it, and it made her shiver deep inside. "Why would you risk yourself for me?"

Because he hated her, and it made no sense. But he was here, offering to do just that. Or maybe he planned to open the door and let them have her...

Ivy shook her head. That wasn't Dane's style. He really was here to protect her.

"It's what I do," he said, shrugging.

Heat blossomed in her cheeks. "So it's the job. No other reason."

His blue eyes were steady. "That's right."

She pushed her long hair back over her shoulder and took a sip of water. Her fingers still trembled, though not as badly as before. She shouldn't have missed the target when she'd fired her weapon.

She'd been distracted. That had to be the issue—and what was distracting her was standing a few feet away and looking as delicious and tempting as ever.

"I still don't understand why it had to be you. Any of those men could watch my back—and it would be a lot less awkward."

"And what if it was more so? You're a gorgeous woman, Ivy. Another man might be distracted by you—and that could prove dangerous, don't you think?"

She heard what he didn't say—that *he* would not be

distracted at all.

"Not every man on earth is attracted to me, Dane. Not to mention, several of those guys are in relationships."

"That doesn't stop some."

A sharpness pierced her. "Would it have stopped you?"

The instant she said it, she regretted it. It was too personal—and too far in the past to even think about.

He straightened, his expression hardening. "When I was married to you, you were the only woman in my life. I'd have never broken the vows I made to you. Never."

Her heart thumped and her stomach tightened. "I shouldn't have asked. It doesn't matter anymore, does it?"

He came around the kitchen island and stalked toward her. But he stopped before he reached her, and her body trembled with excitement. God, if he would only sweep her up into his arms and—

No.

"It matters to me. It matters if you think my integrity is so meaningless to me that I'd have thrown it away the first time we were apart."

"I didn't say that." Her voice was little more than a whisper.

"You didn't have to. But the one thing you never seemed to understand is that I'm not like your father. He might have screwed around on your mother before he left, but I'd have never done that to you. Our marriage vows meant something to me."

She wanted to reach out and touch him. Wanted, more than anything, to dial back the clock and return to a time when there wasn't so much anger and hurt between them.

But that was impossible. Ivy dropped her gaze to the floor, her chest aching with unshed tears and a truckload of regrets.

"I'm sorry, Dane."

He took a step toward her—and then he blew out a breath and turned away, put distance between them. She looked up again, watched him retreat. Her heart hurt in a way it hadn't in a very long time. It was like someone had ripped the bandage off a wound just when it was starting to heal.

"Come on," Dane said over his shoulder. "We've got a team meeting to attend."

TEN

HE MUST HAVE BEEN INSANE to agree to stay in the same space with Ivy. Dane leaned against the wall in the bungalow they were meeting in and listened to Matt and Big Mac talk about the plan. It was a little strange not being in charge of an op for once, but these guys were good. In fact, they were so good that his mind was mostly on Ivy.

She was sitting on a chair a few feet away, one leg crossed demurely over the other, the slit in her dress revealing a tanned calf and part of a thigh. A couple of the other guys glanced at her from time to time, and it made Dane crazy.

It shouldn't make him feel anything at all, and that pissed him off even more. Why did he care who looked at his ex-wife or what she did with that sweet little body of hers anyway? He hadn't made love to her in years, and he knew she hadn't been celibate. Neither had he.

But right now, if he could strip her naked and explore every inch of her body with his tongue and fingers and cock, he'd be a happy man.

Which was crazy, because Ivy didn't make him happy at all. She knotted him up inside, made him feel like his skin was too tight, like if he didn't do something physical —fuck, punch something, run until he was exhausted— he'd explode.

He thought of the conversation he'd had with Matt earlier when the other man had taken him aside.

"I realize asking you to stay with her isn't ideal," Matt said, *"but I get the impression pairing her up with another operator would make it worse for you."*

Dane scoffed. "Don't know why you'd think that. We're divorced. Ivy can do what she pleases."

Matt looked at him for a long moment. "My best friend growing up was a girl. We went everywhere together, did everything—and then we hit high school and things got weird. I did shit I shouldn't have done. She did shit too. It was a bad time in my life. I didn't want her for my own, but I didn't want anyone else to have her either. Then I left town. Didn't see her for ten years."

"So what happened when you saw her again?"

Matt grinned and put his hand over his heart like a love-struck girl. "I'm marrying her, man. Can't live without her."

"Can you do that, Dane?"

Dane gave himself a mental shake. Everyone was looking at him. Everyone except Ivy. She was studying her lap and her tightly clasped hands.

"Can you repeat that?" he asked.

Matt looked amused. "Sure. I need a happy couple to check out our friends with ties to the Freedom Force at the local nightclub. Dinner, dancing, observing who comes and goes. Can you and Ivy do that? Or should I assign someone else in your place?"

"Yeah, I can do it. Ivy?"

She glanced up, seemingly startled that he'd spoken to her. Her dark eyes fixed on his, and then she looked away. "Yes, I can do it with Dane."

Do it with Dane.

Jesus, the pictures that brought up in his head.

"Good. Y'all can go tonight." Matt lifted an eyebrow. "I guess I don't have to explain that we need you to be a *happy* couple, right? You don't have to do anything except smile at each other and pretend you're dating. No need to carry it too far."

"Got it," Dane said.

"This is bullshit." Ace had finally decided to speak. "Ivy's my partner. I should be the one with her over there."

Ivy turned to him and put a hand on his arm. "It's okay. This isn't our op, and we need to do what we can to support it. Besides, I trust Dane."

He could hear the hesitation in her tone and his gut clenched. She didn't fully trust him. She never had. That was part of the problem.

"You trust him? After what he put you through?"

Dane really wanted to knock this guy's head off. Ivy stiffened, and her mouth set in a straight line.

"Not now, Ace."

Her partner glared daggers at Dane. "Fine, chica. Your choice. But don't say I didn't warn you."

"Look," Matt said, "I need a HOT operator out there, not two DEA agents who've never done this kind of mission before. It's Ivy and someone from HOT, though I don't much care who at this point—unless two of you fuckers want to pretend to be a gay couple. We can do that too."

Flash yawned. "All right, all right. I'll let Viking ogle my ass for the cause. But no cuddling, frogman. Not on a first date anyway."

Nick "Brandy" Brandon snorted. Fiddler rolled his eyes. Sam "Knight Rider" McKnight chuckled. Ace's head came up, his eyes flashing at the banter, but Dane had no idea what the fuck that was about. And he didn't care.

"It's okay. Ivy and I got this," Dane said. Because first of all he wasn't playing gay with Flash, and second he couldn't stand the thought of someone else with their hands on Ivy. It was simply too much to process—and Matt somehow knew it, the fucker. "Ivy?"

Her mouth tightened. "Yep, got it. Already said so, didn't I?"

The team talked for another fifteen minutes, and then Matt dismissed them all once the plan was set. Dane and Ivy would go on a date. The rest of the guys would spread out and find the other suspects while Flash and Knight Rider went to the marina to watch for any activity out there. Matt, Big Mac, and Billy "the Kid" Blake—the computer whiz—would stay here to monitor the comm feeds and pass on any information.

Dane walked Ivy back to their bungalow. The path through the resort was lush, planted with tropical foliage and studded with cute little bridges and swans and shit. He supposed it was a romantic place, the kind of spot where couples honeymooned or spent anniversaries.

And yet he kept an eye on the surroundings for danger, especially since the sun was beginning to set and the path was darkening in spots.

"You have to forgive Ace," Ivy said, and Dane glanced at her, surprised.

"Actually, I don't."

She sighed. "He's protective, that's all. He's a good guy and he cares. I might have talked a bit too much about why I'm never getting married again."

"Are you fucking him?"

She stopped and pivoted toward him, her skin mottled with fresh color. "What kind of question is that? And what business is it of yours anyway?"

"It's the kind of question a man wonders when another man keeps acting like a jealous prick. It's my business because I'm prepared to jump in front of a bullet for you. I'd like to know if one of those bullets might be Ace's."

"Ace has been my partner for two years. And he'd rather fuck you than me. So what do you say now, asshole?"

Dane blinked. "He's gay?"

Ivy looked angrier than he'd ever seen her. "Is that a problem for you?"

"No. Why would it be?"

He honestly didn't care who the dude fucked—unless it was Ivy, and then he cared very much for some stupid-ass reason. But now he found himself pretty damn happy that Ace wasn't Ivy's lover—and apparently didn't want to be. He also understood now why Ace had seemed annoyed at the team meeting. The banter was typical guy stuff—but when you *were* gay, maybe that kind of thing hurt in a way.

Ivy huffed out a breath and then turned and started back up the path toward the bungalow. Dane didn't have to hurry to catch up—his stride was much longer than hers. Her nose was in the air as she walked. When she reached the door, he put an arm up to block her from going inside.

Because of their height difference, his arm went across her chest. Her soft breasts pressed against his skin. She squeaked and took a hasty step back. But not before the feel of her was imprinted on his brain.

"I have to go in first," he said, trying to be all business.

Her face was red but she nodded. Dane pulled his gun and swiped the keycard. Then he went inside and did a sweep of the interior. When he'd determined it was clear, he went back for Ivy.

She was standing against the wall outside, facing the path leading up to the bungalow. He'd bet she had a gun strapped under her dress, against her leg. The thought of cool metal lying against her skin, taking on her heat, made his cock stir with interest.

Ivy hadn't been in the DEA when they'd been married. Neither of them had carried weapons on a regular basis then. They were different people now. Darker people. People who'd seen a lot of shit and who'd faced death in the line of duty.

It bothered him that Ivy had become the sort of person who faced danger. He'd never pictured that for her, though maybe he should have. She'd always been tough and determined, and she had a keen sense of justice.

"It's clear," he said, and she nodded and joined him inside. "Are you armed?"

He needed to know. And maybe he wanted to know because it excited him to think she was wearing a weapon tucked somewhere out of sight.

"Yes."

He let his gaze skim her body-hugging dress. "I hate

to ask where it might be."

"Then don't."

His eyes met hers. There was a flicker of something there—but then it went away and she looked determined. Professional. She opened her purse and lifted a Glock so he could see the grip.

Shit, not what he'd pictured.

Ivy laughed, and it startled him. "Where did you think I'd put it? Between my legs? That would be a bitch to walk around with."

Yeah, but the thought of a gun there...

"Oh hell, you *were* picturing it, weren't you? Men."

Dane held up his hands. "Guilty as charged. I'm shallow that way."

"You really don't care that Ace is gay?"

Talk about left field. He'd nearly forgotten Ace Martin as he'd thought about a gun nestled between Ivy's thighs.

"No, Ivy. I don't care."

She lifted her shoulders and shrugged them as if working out a knot. "Some guys do. He's not in the closet, precisely, but doing what we do... he's not exactly out of it either."

"Understood."

"You aren't going to say anything to the others?"

"It's not my place to discuss Ace's sex life. Even if he thinks it's his right to comment on you and me and how we fit into this mission."

Ivy had the grace to look embarrassed. "I might have gotten drunk a couple of times in the past. And I might have spoken at length about my asshole ex-husband and how he'd made it hard to trust other men. It happens."

Dane felt as though she'd jabbed him in the gut. "It's not me who made it hard for you to trust men, Ivy. You were already that way when we met."

Her jaw tightened. "Yes, but you're the first one I tried to trust. When it didn't work out... well, let's just say I'm not too inclined to try again."

He wanted to pull her into his arms and hold her. Stroke her hair and tell her she deserved better than that. But he didn't have that right.

"Blame me if you need to," he said softly. "But we both know it takes two to fuck up a relationship."

ELEVEN

IVY SANK INTO THE DARK rounded booth against the wall and let her gaze slide around the room. The nightclub was a bit more upscale than she'd expected, with chrome and steel fixtures, marble-topped tables, and mirrors placed strategically around the space. The music was modern and couples gyrated out on the floor while waitresses in tight skirts and low-cut tops moved among the tables and took orders.

"Not too many people here," Ivy said.

"It's early. Give it two hours and it'll be packed."

Ivy let her gaze meet Dane's. As usual, a spark flared to life in her belly. She was getting really tired of that spark, dammit.

"I really don't want to be here in two hours."

He shrugged. "Not sure we have a choice, baby."

"Don't call me baby," she ground out.

Dane gave her that lopsided grin that made her heart skip a beat. Then he reached for her hand. "We're happy, remember?"

When he lifted her hand and brushed his mouth over

her knuckles, she thought she might come right then and there because the sensation of pleasure racing through her was so intense. It was like there was a string between her hand and her clit and every brush of his lips against her skin tugged that string tighter.

Ivy shifted and carefully extracted her hand. "No need to overdo it," she murmured as she picked up the menu and studied it.

Dane slid into the center of the booth and tugged her over until she was right up against him. Then he put an arm around her, one broad hand resting on her hip, and pretended to look at the menu. Or maybe he *was* looking at the menu. Honest to God, she couldn't think. Her brain had short-circuited.

"We're staying at a romantic resort in the Keys, Ivy. We're supposed to overdo it." His voice in her ear was a growl that sent a shiver down her spine.

"If I'd thought for two seconds you were going to use this particular assignment as an excuse to put your hands all over me, I'd have told Matt I couldn't do it."

Dane leaned back in the booth, his gaze hooded as he studied her. She could feel her pulse pounding recklessly in her throat, and she hoped like hell he couldn't see it.

But she should have known that was a fruitless wish.

His mouth curled in a smile. "Or maybe that's why you agreed, Ivy. Maybe you like having my hands on you. You used to."

"*Used to* being the key phrase here." Oh, why did she have to sound so breathless when she said it?

He brushed his fingertips along her bare arm, and she shuddered before she could contain the reaction.

"I'm not going to lie to you. I'm hard—and it's got

72

nothing to do with *used to*."

Ivy's breath shortened. "Don't say things like that, Dane."

"Why not? Because it makes you wet?"

Ivy closed her eyes. Dear heaven, yes, she was wet. Wet and hot and aching for what she knew this man could give her. But sex had never been their problem—and if she went down that road with him, where would it lead this time? How could it possibly end well?

"How is this helping us do what we came here to do?" she forced out. "We have work to do, and sex isn't a part of it. Besides, aren't you just a little bit worried about your career if you start banging random agents on the job?"

Dane's gaze was serious. "You aren't a random agent, Ivy. And no, I'm not worried about my career. This—you and me—is different."

Her pulse thumped. "I'm not sure Mendez would agree. In fact, I bet he'd be pissed as hell if we let something escape our attention because we can't concentrate on the job."

"Who said I can't concentrate?"

A waitress appeared at their table before Ivy could answer. "What can I get for you two?"

She was blond and buxom, and she gave Dane a slow once-over. Ivy found herself wanting to smack the woman with her menu.

"I'll have a sparkling water with a lemon slice," Ivy said with annoyance.

"And you, hon?" the woman said to Dane.

He grinned, of course. "I'll have a Dos Equis Amber. We'll also take an order of those ahi sliders you got, and some truffle fries. Make that two truffle fries. My girl can eat a whole order by herself."

"Sure thing, hon," the woman said before giving him a wink and turning on her heel.

"Two orders of truffle fries? How do you know I even like such a beast?"

"I don't. But you used to eat all my fries—or did you forget?"

Ivy's cheeks heated. "I didn't forget. But I used to have the metabolism to burn them off. No more. You're wasting your money."

"They're fries, Ivy. If you don't eat them, I think I can take the hit to my wallet."

He made her want to laugh, but she was determined not to.

"Why are you drinking? We're supposed to be observing."

He reached up and caught a lock of her hair in his fingers. Then he twirled it around his index finger while giving her a sexy look that made her ache.

"I can nurse one beer and observe. If we're both drinking water and you're glaring at me like you are right now, we're not going to fool anyone."

She looked down at the menu still in her hand and pushed it across the table. He was right, but damn, how was it that he could be so nonchalant about this whole thing? Her belly was doing backflips at his proximity, and her nerve pathways were lit up like a fireworks display on a summer night.

Yet he seemed so cool and untouched. And arrogant. Definitely arrogant with that smirk and knowing gaze.

"What if I didn't want ahi sliders?"

"Then order something else."

She sat back against the seat, and he pulled her in close, his arm going around her shoulders. She told herself it was part of their cover, but her heart hammered and her skin sizzled and her brain couldn't think of anything but satin sheets and naked bodies.

"So was I right?" he asked, his breath hot in her ear.

A shiver slid down her spine. "Right about what?"

The club wasn't too busy, and she had a clear view to the bar. Their target was supposed to be a bartender, but he hadn't shown up yet. She studied the people at the bar, the man behind the bar. If she could concentrate on the job, she could get through this.

"Do I make you wet?"

Ivy wanted to whimper. Hell yes, he made her wet. And hot. Where the hell was her water?

"Does it matter?" she croaked.

"It does to me."

He pushed her hair back, and then his lips were on her neck, nibbling so lightly she could scream. Ivy gasped—and subtly offered him more by tilting her throat toward him.

It was an instinctive reaction, and she regretted it immediately.

Or did she? Because she wasn't precisely pulling away, was she?

"What do you want me to say? Yes? Would that make you happy?"

"The only thing that would make me happy is burying my cock inside you," he whispered.

"Dane," she choked, torn between throwing caution to the wind to have a wild night with him and pushing him away and telling him to keep his dirty thoughts to himself. "We're here for a reason. And if you keep talking to me like that, I won't be able to focus."

He nipped her, not hard, but enough to make a little sting of pleasure slide down into her pussy. Then he eased back and leaned against the seat again.

She turned to look at him. "That's it? No argument?"

His eyes glittered. "No. You admitted you want me too. That's all I need to hear."

"I didn't say that."

He grinned. "Sure you did." He slid his fingers over her shoulder again and she shuddered. "You said you couldn't focus. That's enough for me. Because you're affected, Ivy. You want me every bit as much as I want you. This thing between us is like lighting a match in a fireworks factory and hoping you don't drop it."

She wanted to deny it… and yet she couldn't. They hadn't seen each other in over four years. And now, after only two days in each other's company, she was constantly thinking about what being in bed with him felt like.

She'd had sex since Dane. But none of it had been as *good* as sex with Dane had been. She'd told herself after a particularly disappointing encounter over a year ago—the last time she'd had sex, in fact—that she was idolizing that part of her life with Dane. That it couldn't possibly be true. No man was that fabulous in bed, and no sexual encounter was that hot and perfect.

Ivy swallowed. "Then I guess we better not drop it, right?"

TWELVE

THEY STAYED AT THE NIGHTCLUB for three hours. Dane nursed two beers during that time, and Ivy finally agreed to have a glass of wine. She drank exactly half of it. They ate and watched the crowd and the bar. He kept in contact with mission control throughout the night, but their target didn't show up. Dane didn't know how the other guys were doing, though he hoped it was going better for them.

Around midnight, Matt sent a message and told him to wind it up. Dane signaled for the check and then helped Ivy out of the booth.

He put his arm around her waist and ushered her from the club. The minute they got outside, the night breeze hit them, bringing with it the smells of tropical flowers and the salty tang of the ocean. Ivy stepped out of his embrace, and he clenched his fist as he forced himself not to reach out and drag her back into the circle of his arm.

He liked having her there. More than he should. He knew all the reasons Ivy was wrong for him, and yet he'd spent the entire night fighting an erection because she was so damn close and smelled so good.

And then there was the dress she was wearing. It was the same one from earlier, the same body-hugging silky fabric, but she'd added a pair of high heels. The way her legs peeked out from the slit when she walked nearly had him drooling.

She wasn't tall, but he knew those legs would wrap around his waist just right. He really shouldn't be thinking those thoughts, shouldn't be prodding her and asking her if she was as wet as he was hard, because there was no time for this kind of thing right now.

He couldn't seem to help himself though. Whenever she gave him an opening, whenever she seemed flustered at his nearness or he heard that little hitch in her breath when his fingers skimmed her bare arm, he couldn't seem to stop.

He'd told her he wasn't concerned about hurting his career because this thing between them was different. But the truth was he knew it wasn't a good idea to lust after his mission partner even if she was his ex-wife. No commanding officer in the history of the world was going to be thrilled with a soldier or sailor who couldn't keep his dick in his pants during a critical operation.

Dane's phone buzzed in his pocket. It was Matt.

Slight detour. Swing by the marina on your way back. Three of our suspects there with a boat. Getting ready to go out. Flash & KR can't get close enough. Maybe you can.

Dane texted a one word reply: *Copy.* "Let's take a walk down to the marina," he said to Ivy.

She turned her head. "Now? It's midnight, Dane."

He reached for her hand and glanced around at the street. There were people out, drinking, carousing, and having a good time. It was definitely a tourist town.

"I know, babe. But you know how much I like boats."

She looked at him for a long minute. And then she nodded. "Okay."

"You gonna be all right in those shoes?" he asked as they walked.

"It's not that far."

"You let me know if it gets to be too much. I'll give you a piggyback ride."

She snorted. "I'll keep that in mind."

They headed down an alley and cut over to another street along the waterfront. There were several marinas on Emerald Key, but this one was run by one of their suspects. Omar Baz was a citizen now, but his parents had emigrated from Afghanistan when he was ten. He had suspected ties to radical groups, though he'd never done anything illegal. He had, however, made several trips to the Middle East—specifically Qu'rim and Acamar—over the past few years. That wasn't a crime, and yet it was somewhat suspicious considering his business didn't take him there.

Dane led Ivy down the plank dock and toward the shuttered restaurant on the water. The sound of laughter came from a boat parked in a slip where a group partied hard. Not the boat Flash was talking about, probably.

"What are we looking for?"

"Nothing special."

"Dane." She was frowning at him like he was a kid caught in a lie.

He pulled her in close and put his arms around her. She stiffened for a moment, and then she went soft in his arms as he lowered his head and nuzzled her ear.

"Boat," he said, breathing her in. "Getting ready to go out."

She lifted a hand to his cheek, and a lightning bolt of need shot to his groin.

"Okay."

The sound of voices came across the water and hit their ears. It wasn't the laughing people this time. The language was foreign. He couldn't tell what it was though.

"It's not Spanish," Ivy said as if she'd read his mind.

"Come on."

She went with him down the dock, toward the sound. They moved slowly, feeling their way along based on the tone of the voices. A change would mean they'd been seen or heard. But the men kept talking like nothing had interrupted their conversation.

Dane led Ivy to the railing of the restaurant. The deck was higher here and looked down on another part of the marina. A light shone along one narrow arm of docking. Three men stood together, smoking and gesturing toward a boat.

"Can you see the name of the boat?" Ivy asked.

"Too dark."

"Then we need to get down there."

He grabbed her hand as she turned and started to walk toward the stairs leading down. "Too dangerous."

"And what we're searching for isn't?"

She had him there, but still. He wasn't going to risk taking her closer. If he could get her to the bungalow and make sure she was secure, he could double back.

"We know which slip. That's enough."

"No, it's not." She took his hand and a jolt rolled through him. "Can you act drunk?"

"What?"

"Drunk, Dane. Can you act the part?"

"That's not what I was saying 'what' about. You aren't going down there."

Ivy sidled up to him then, laid her palms on his chest before sliding them up and over his shoulders. "Yes, I am, sugar. With or without you. Now, I suggest you act drunk and follow my lead. Can you do that?"

He let his hands slide around to her ass. It was cheap of him, but shit, she was gorgeous and she made him horny.

"What do I get for the trouble?"

Because he knew she wasn't going to let this go, and if he went along with her, he could still control the situation.

"You get to touch my ass like you're doing without me ripping your head off."

He almost laughed. Then he squeezed her bottom appreciatively. "Might be worth it. Be more worth it if you'd let me kiss your ass."

She patted his cheek. "One thing at a time, honey. One thing at a time."

THIRTEEN

IVY TUGGED DANE TOWARD THE stairs. She didn't think he would go at first, but he followed her down until they were on the main dock. From there, it was a short walk to the dock that branched down toward where the men were. When they reached the entrance to that dock, she stopped and turned to Dane. He didn't look happy, but at least he was cooperating.

"You ready for this?" she asked.

"As I'll ever be… but Ivy…"

She turned back to him.

"If anyone makes a move toward you, I'm done doing things your way."

Ivy sighed in frustration. "Don't get twitchy on me. No jumping the gun. Make sure they're really going to try to harm me first, okay?"

He snorted. "Haven't you ever heard the saying shoot first and ask questions later? If I wait, it could be too late."

"I've heard the saying… but let's not start shooting anything without extreme provocation, all right?"

He sighed unconvincingly. "Yeah, all right."

She started down the dock and Dane walked behind her. The men were still smoking, still talking, and hadn't yet noticed them. But the click of Ivy's shoes on the boards made them look up suddenly. One man reached behind his back.

Ivy knew it was now or never. If she didn't do something, Dane would go all superhero in about three seconds. And that would ruin any chance they had of finding out information that could lead them to the submarine.

Ivy giggled like she had a head full of air and took Dane's hand, her heart thrumming with adrenaline and a touch of excitement. He stiffened slightly, but she pushed him against a pillar and plastered herself to him. For a split second, she thought he wouldn't cooperate. But then his hands went around her and her breath shortened as she found herself flattened against the full length of Dane's body.

Oh God, what had she been thinking? This was insanity. Not the part where they came out here to find the boat's name, but the part where she let Dane hold her. It was like she'd been subjected to sensory deprivation for years and now everything was lighting up at once.

If this lasted too long, she'd melt into a puddle on the planks below her feet.

"This is a private dock," a rough voice said. "You need to go."

Ivy looked at the man who'd spoken. Then she giggled again and stumbled against Dane for good measure. "We rented a boat. Isn't that right, pumpkin?"

Dane grunted. "Fuck yeah, we did."

"There are no boats for rent here," the man said.

"Sure there are. We rented one... and we can't find it.

But we really need to because..." She wrapped her leg around Dane's hip. She didn't miss the burgeoning erection that pressed into her center or the strong urge she had to ride that bump until she came. "We have to go to bed."

Dane groaned softly. "'S here, babe. I know it is. Need to get you naked before I e'splode."

He lowered his mouth to her neck, pushing her hair aside so he could suck the skin of her throat. Ivy wanted to whimper.

One of the men laughed, and the other said something that sounded like a curse before turning back to the boat they'd left. The one who'd been doing all the talking stayed, but he didn't pull a weapon.

"Sorry, but you're on the wrong dock. You didn't rent a boat from anyone here." Laughter floated across the marina from the party boat. The man tipped his chin. "That's probably where you need to be. Follow that noise and you'll find your boat."

"Are you sure?" Ivy asked, infusing her voice with disappointment and a touch of helium. Speak in a high little-girl voice and men didn't take you seriously. She'd learned that over the years and used it to her advantage when necessary.

"Positive, lady. This is a working dock. Nothing but fishing boats here. You don't want to get naked on one of those, I assure you."

"But maybe it's down there." She pointed past where the men were gathered. Their boat wasn't far, but she didn't know if Dane could see the name yet or not. She couldn't, but she was shorter than he was.

"It's not down there, lady." The man practically growled it.

"Come on, babe. Think the dude's right." Dane belched and stumbled back the way they'd come, holding on to her hand and tugging her with him.

"But, honey," Ivy wailed. "You promised."

"You need to turn that girl over your knee," the man called after them as they walked away. He must have said something to the other men because they laughed, the sound following Dane and Ivy up the dock.

He didn't let her hand go until they were on the street and he'd gone around a corner into a tight alley between two shops that were closed for the night, pushing her behind him. Then he pulled his gun and waited.

But no one was following them. He holstered the gun and stepped away from her, letting her breathe without smelling his scent for a change.

"That was fucking insane," he said.

"But it worked. Please tell me it worked."

He grinned. "*Bad Medicine.*"

"That's the name of the boat?"

"Yep." He took his phone out and sent a text, presumably to the team. Then he put it away and shook his head. "You're crazy, Ivy. Reckless."

"That wasn't reckless, Dane. It was a plan and it worked."

His eyes glittered as he took her elbows and tugged her in close. "That's not the kind of reckless I was talking about, babe."

Her breath didn't want to fill her lungs. Her heart hammered hard enough to make her light-headed. Her body sizzled and sparked with need.

"We had to look harmless," she said, forcing the words past the huge knot in her throat. "It was necessary."

"So is this." Dane pulled her up on her tiptoes—and then he crushed his mouth down on hers.

FOURTEEN

IVY MOANED AS HER MOUTH opened and Dane's tongue invaded. Her arms went around his neck and her body arched into his before she realized what she was doing.

But kissing Dane was the best kind of insanity. She'd forgotten how good it was, how the slide of his tongue against hers made her limbs weak and her skin hot. She knew she should push him away, but she was like a woman dying of thirst and Dane was the first drink of water she'd had in ages.

His hands slid down her body, over the fabric of her dress, and then he cupped her ass and brought her in tightly against his groin. He was hard. So big and hard.

Dane turned their bodies then, walked her backward until she hit the plank wall of a building. Then he grasped her thigh, his hand gliding beneath the slit in her dress, and pulled her leg up and around his hip.

Ivy didn't stop him. She didn't want to stop him.

"Ivy, fuck, you feel so good," Dane groaned against her mouth.

"Don't stop," she moaned. "Please don't stop."

Her nipples were hard points and her skin burned. It was as if someone had held a candle flame too close. She was hot almost to the point of pain, but not quite. Hot and itchy and achy. Parts of her that had been dormant too long flared to life.

Dane's fingers strayed over her hip, down the curve of her ass, and then between her legs. Right over the tiny thong she'd worn beneath her dress. Ivy gasped as he stroked his fingers back and forth over the hot dampness of her panties.

"You're so wet," he groaned. "I need to be in here, Ivy. I need to fill you with my cock and take you hard."

"*Yes.*"

That was all the encouragement he needed. Dane grasped her thong and tugged it down even while she reached for his belt with trembling fingers. Somehow she got the belt undone, and then Dane unbuttoned and unzipped his jeans before shoving her dress up and cupping her ass in both of his broad hands.

Ivy put her legs around his waist, her mouth crushing down on his, her heart pounding hard and strong as his cock slid against the wet seam of her sex. This was every hot fantasy she'd ever had, every bittersweet memory of the months she'd spent with Dane.

But she couldn't stop. It was almost as if she needed one last time with him to get him out of her system. As if the way they'd parted over four years ago needed an epilogue to complete it.

Warning bells echoed in her head, but her body told her brain to get lost. Thoughts weren't welcome at this particular party.

The head of his cock slipped between the slick lips of her pussy. Ivy moaned deep in her throat, and Dane flexed his hips and pushed deeper still, holding her hard against the wall as he entered her fully.

She was caught between Dane and an uneven surface that pressed into her back almost uncomfortably.

She didn't care.

Dane held her ass and started to move, his thrusts hard and sure. Their mouths fused together, and their breaths came out in pants and grunts.

Ivy put her hands on his jaw, held him while she kissed him with all the passion and pain she'd been holding in for so long. This was bliss. Heaven. Everything she'd ever wanted when they'd been together.

Everything she'd missed since they'd divorced.

Dane's fingers dug into her ass. Ivy tightened her legs around him, shifting her hips so that her clit rode against the base of his cock. Fire streaked through her body, into her blood and bones, twisting and turning in her belly, tightening everything around the physical connection between her and Dane.

She tore her mouth from his as the pleasure spiraled out of control like the turning of a spring. Everything grew impossibly tight as he fucked her harder. It was too fast, too intense—and there was no stopping it.

The stubble of his jaw scraped against her as he put his mouth to her ear and nibbled on her earlobe. "You're amazing, Ivy. So hot and beautiful. Missed you. Missed this."

"Yes... Dane, Dane—oh, damn."

She plunged over the edge with a sharp cry as her body splintered apart on wave after wave of body-tingling pleasure. Dane captured her mouth to smother the sounds she made, but she honestly didn't care who heard her right this second. She was beyond caring.

Dane's breath came faster as he pumped into her—and then he pulled away at the last second, spilling himself on the ground with a groan.

Their breathing was harsh in the stillness of the alley. Slowly, Ivy's senses came back to her—and embarrassment was key among them, as she'd known it would be. She looked around the alley with wild eyes, worried someone was watching them, but no one was there.

Dane set her down, the warmth of his body leaving hers as he stepped back and fixed his jeans. When he looked up at her, it was with shuttered eyes. Her heart twisted to see such naked regret on his face.

"I'm sorry."

Ivy swallowed. She pushed away from the wall and straightened her dress. Her legs were weak and her body still tingled from the incredible orgasm. She hadn't come like that in a very long time, and a part of her didn't regret it at all.

But anger kindled in her belly, a slow blaze that warmed her from the inside out.

"Don't apologize," she snapped. "It makes me feel like I forced you into something against your will."

He blinked. "That's an odd way to feel if I'm the one apologizing, isn't it?"

"No, not when you say you're sorry like someone made you do the worst thing imaginable. Fucking your ex-wife... what is the world coming to?"

"That's not what I meant." He rubbed a hand over his forehead. "I meant that I'm sorry for pushing you, for not being able to control myself—and for not protecting you in all the ways I'm supposed to protect you."

Ivy had to think about that for a second. She got the part where he felt responsible for her safety—and then she sucked in a deep breath and huffed it out again when she understood the other part. "I'm still on the pill. It's fine."

He nodded, but he stood there like a kid who'd been caught in the cookie jar. He looked... chastened. And maybe a little angry.

Ivy couldn't look at him another moment. She spun on her heel and started up the alley. Tears blurred her vision, but she dashed them away and kept going.

Dane caught her arm and forced her to stop.

"Don't," he said. "Don't walk away like it was nothing."

She spun and glared at him. "I don't know what it was. It wasn't nothing. But it wasn't anything either. It can't be."

He snorted. "Because if we know anything, it's how to take good sex and fuck it up beyond repair."

Her heart ached. "Is that all it was between us?"

He lifted his head and looked into the distance. His jaw was tight. "You know better than that. You meant the world to me, Ivy. I thought I meant the world to you."

She swallowed the lump in her throat. "You did." The words came out as a whisper, but he heard them.

He shook his head. "No, it's too late for that, babe. If it had been true, you wouldn't have let me go."

"How was I supposed to stop you, Dane?" she cried. "I'd given you everything, and it wasn't enough. *I* wasn't enough."

FIFTEEN

SHE STOOD THERE WITH A world of pain in her eyes, and Dane felt like something was breaking inside him. He didn't know what it was, but it hurt, which was surprising considering he'd thought his days of hurting over this woman were finished.

Apparently he'd been wrong. She still had the ability to gut him with her words—and he still had no idea how to fix it.

He wanted to say more. He searched his head for the words, but nothing would come. He knew from experience that there was no way to fix this. It wasn't as simple as a few words, a new understanding. It was complex and had deep roots that he'd never been able to dislodge.

"It's late. We should get a taxi," he said.

Ivy didn't look at him, and his heart kicked with fresh pain. *Tell her she was enough for you, idiot.*

But he couldn't seem to do it. The words would sound hollow and she would know it. No matter how much he meant them, she wouldn't believe.

Dane flagged a taxi on the main street and helped Ivy

inside. Rather than shut the door and go around, he made her scoot over. He wasn't taking any chances with leaving her alone and walking around to the other side, even though no one had followed them from the dock. He'd already fucked up enough tonight, and he had to get his head back in the game.

The ride to the resort didn't take long. They didn't speak along the way. Ivy turned her head and looked out the window, shutting him out. Dane clenched his hand into a fist and rhythmically thumped his leg.

This whole evening was a clusterfuck. What had he been thinking anyway? Taking her like that in an alley where anyone could stumble upon them? Where they could have been caught unaware by an assailant?

He hadn't done the best job of protecting her then, had he?

All he'd meant to do was kiss her, but he should have known it wouldn't end there. It couldn't. When he and Ivy touched, the world faded. It had always been that way. He'd have thought he knew better by now, but in truth he was still pretty stunned that all he had to do was touch her and he lost his head.

He'd thought he had it under control in the bar. He'd touched and teased because he could, because he'd wanted to make her acknowledge there was still heat between them. He'd told her they were like a fireworks factory, but he'd known the whole time that he had control of the matches.

Huh, some control. He'd gotten just as burned as she had. And he'd forgotten everything while he'd done it— her safety, the mission, his career.

He paid the driver and they got out at the resort's

main building. It was nearly one o'clock in the morning, but there were still people at the open-air bar. Dane put his hand on the small of Ivy's back and steered her down the path toward their bungalow. He didn't miss the way she flinched when his fingertips grazed her.

He scanned their surroundings, but nothing was out of place. When they reached the bungalow, he went in first and did his check, then retrieved her from the porch. She looked annoyed, but he wasn't sure if it was because he'd made her stand outside or because of everything that had happened in the alley.

He didn't know how to fix that, but he knew he couldn't keep avoiding it.

He stood with his hands shoved in his jeans pockets and watched her. She set her purse down and finally looked up at him.

Her green eyes drew him in like always. He'd never been so affected by a woman in his life as he had Ivy.

"Say something, Ivy."

She shrugged. "I don't know what to say to you anymore."

"Did you ever regret what happened between us and wish it had been different?"

He thought she might not answer, but then she tipped her chin up. "All the time. I threw myself into work, hoping it would ease the ache of your being gone. And it did, after a time."

He blew out a breath. "Did you really think I wanted to join the SEALs because you weren't enough for me? That I was trying to get away from you?"

Her head bowed as she fiddled with the neckline of her dress, straightening it even though it didn't need to be.

"I was prepared for you to join the Navy. You'd told me that was your plan. And yes, that terrified me because my father was in the Navy and he got addicted to being at sea. But the SEALs…"

She closed her eyes for a moment. When she looked at him again, her eyes glittered. It took him a moment to realize those were tears.

"I knew I would lose you to the adrenaline rush of being a SEAL. I wasn't wrong."

"That's not how it happened," he growled in frustration. "You gave me an ultimatum."

"And you chose the SEALs over me."

He swore. Explosively. "Do you really think ultimatums are how relationships work, Ivy? Or should work? What if I'd said it was me or the DEA? What then?"

She put her hand to her forehead, covered her eyes. Then she dropped it again and stared at him. "I think the point is that what we wanted from each other and what we wanted from life was different. It was never going to work out, Dane. Maybe it's good we realized that early."

"Jesus H. Christ, Ivy—that's bullshit and you know it. It's an excuse because you don't like messy emotions. You've spent your life avoiding being close to anyone. Thinking that if you hold a part of yourself separate you can survive it when they leave you."

She blinked. And then her face reddened. "And how are you any different? You were raised by emotionally distant parents. Because of them, you don't trust that anyone can really love you or care what happens to you."

It was his turn to blink. Anger welled up inside him, fresh and hot. It was always like this with Ivy. She knew right where to hit him, how to bring him to his emotional knees. Yeah, he came from a "perfect" home—the kind of home where his father was the king of everything and his mother was the model officer's wife. He'd had to be the perfect kid—get the best grades, play all the sports, excel at every fucking thing he ever did, be polite to everyone— but no matter how hard he worked, how hard he tried, his mother patted him on the head and sent him on his way. She didn't hug him or tell him she loved him. He couldn't ever remember that from when he'd been a kid. By the time he'd been a teenager, he hadn't cared anymore.

And his father—yeah, best not to even go there. His father was married to his work. A stranger who exerted military discipline at home and expected there to be no drama. Ever. Love? Dane wasn't even sure his father knew what that word meant.

Dane sighed and rubbed his forehead. They'd never gotten anywhere by bringing up the same old shit. "If you could do our relationship over, what would you do differently?"

Her eyes were sad. "I wouldn't have danced with you in the first place."

Pain wrapped around his heart and squeezed. Then he laughed. "I should have known that's what you would say."

"It would have saved us both a lot of pain, don't you think?"

"Maybe so. But then we wouldn't know what it was like to love someone so much it hurt either." He sucked in a breath. "Maybe you're right about me and I do find it hard to trust—but I don't regret trying with you, Ivy. What would I do differently? I'd have chosen you when you gave me that ultimatum."

SIXTEEN

IVY WAS A TREMBLING MESS as she got ready for bed. She wasn't scared and she wasn't mad. But she was jumpy as hell, and every bit of it was because of the man in the next room.

He'd yanked the rug right out from under her feet with his declaration that he wouldn't have left if he had it to do over again. Remarkably, she also felt a strong current of shame at his announcement.

Because he was right that relationships weren't built on ultimatums. She'd been wrong to say that to him, but she'd been so scared and had tried whatever she could think of to make him stay. All she could remember was her mother crying as her father packed his stuff and left for the last time. Her mother had begged, said she would do anything, but he'd pushed her away and told her it was over.

Ivy knew that begging didn't work. So she'd done something reckless—and her recklessness had cost her every bit as much as begging would have.

When he'd asked tonight what she would have done

differently, all she could think was that she could have avoided the pain of a relationship with Dane by rejecting his advance in the first place.

That shamed her too, especially considering how profound what he'd said had been. She put her head in her hands and concentrated on breathing. In, out. In, out. Slowly. If she concentrated, maybe she could stop her heart from racing and her blood from pounding in her veins.

When it didn't work, when turning off the lights and crawling into bed didn't work, she threw off the covers and padded over to the sliding glass doors that opened onto a secluded patio. She couldn't see the ocean from here, but she could hear it and smell it. Maybe it would soothe her enough that she could go to sleep.

Ivy went outside and stood on the edge of the patio, smelling the salt and dampness. It was humid, but she didn't care. She was wearing a long T-shirt—one of Dane's old shirts, in fact—and a pair of panties, which was about as close to naked as she could get for being outdoors.

"You shouldn't be outside."

Ivy jumped at the sound of a male voice—but it was Dane, so she didn't panic. He stood in his open doorway and watched her. She hadn't heard him slide the door back.

"I couldn't sleep."

He sighed. "Me either. I heard your door open."

"You wanted to know what I would do differently," she blurted, her heart racing like mad. "I wouldn't give you an ultimatum. I would trust that everything would be okay. And if it wasn't, then at least we tried."

He stepped outside. He wasn't wearing anything except a pair of dark shorts. The meager light caressed the smooth bumps and planes of his chest, outlining how perfect he was. They'd had sex in an alley, but she hadn't seen his naked chest. Or any part of him, come to think of it. The whole thing had been so frantic and out of control that they'd only bared the essential parts.

She wanted to explore him. Wanted to lick a trail down the center of his body until she could take his cock in her mouth and taste him again.

It was a surprising desire considering how emotionally shattered she'd felt after their recent encounter.

Physically, however, she hadn't felt that good in ages. And she was shocked to learn that she wanted more.

He smiled at her then. A soft, sad smile that made her heart ache.

"Thanks for saying that, Ivy."

It hit her that he thought she was saying it out of a sense of guilt or something. "I mean it, Dane. I… I didn't respond the way I should have the first time. Because you're right that I hold back to protect myself. It's an old habit, and it's not easy to break."

He cocked his head as if considering. "Thanks," he said softly. "I know that wasn't easy for you."

She wrapped her arms around herself as a chill washed over her. It wasn't from the outdoors, but from the emotions that always raged between them when they were in the same room together.

"No, it wasn't. But I know I need to acknowledge what's broken before I can fix it."

"You did good tonight, Ivy. On the dock, I mean. I think you're probably a hell of a DEA agent."

"Thank you." She could feel the heat of his compliment in the tips of her ears. "All I want is to make a difference. To stop others from suffering from the drug trade."

"I think you've made a difference. You may never know some of the people you've helped, but their lives are better because of you and Ace."

Her throat tightened. "I hope so."

"Do you think you can sleep now?"

"Not really. But I'll go back inside since I know you won't go in until I do."

"That's right, honey."

She walked over to the sliding glass door and opened it. Then she stopped and looked at him. She could go to bed alone, and that was probably what she *should* do—but her heart hurt and her emotions boiled and she needed connection with someone. With Dane.

"Wouldn't it be easier to keep me safe if we were in the same room together?"

She could feel the tension rolling from him. "Are you sure about that?"

"Would I have said it if I wasn't?"

"Ivy, I don't know fuck all about what you would do anymore. Maybe you want to torture me and you'll lock your door in my face before I get there. Maybe you'll insist you meant I have to sleep on the floor beside your bed. I honestly have no clue."

"Until tonight, I haven't had sex in over a year. I forgot how much I missed it."

She thought he growled. "You know something? I really don't like hearing about you having sex with someone else. It makes me want to hit something. Hard."

"I didn't give you details."

He took a step toward her. "If you've had sex in less than four and a half years, it's been with someone else. And yeah, that makes me crazy."

"Like you've been celibate."

"Nope."

Ivy shook her head even as jealousy bloomed in her soul. "We're losing the thread of the conversation here."

"No, we definitely aren't. You want to have sex with me because you're feeling deprived. I heard you loud and clear."

Electricity popped beneath her skin. "Is that a problem?"

He laughed low and deep. "It should be… but, no. Not at all."

Her belly tumbled and her pussy tightened. "Well… Good." She stepped into her room. "I'll be waiting for you."

The look he gave her singed her. "If you change your mind before I get there, lock your door. Because if the door isn't locked, Ivy—you're mine. All night long."

SEVENTEEN

HE DIDN'T TAKE LONG TO secure the doors and windows. Ivy was kneeling on the bed, her heart pounding, when the door to her room opened. Dane was silhouetted against the light coming from the microwave clock. Butterflies soared in her stomach.

Why? It wasn't the first time they'd had sex, and she had no reason to be afraid. Except she felt vulnerable in a way she hadn't before, and she couldn't seem to make that feeling go away.

The sensible thing to do would be to send him away. But she couldn't. If she could have done that, she'd have never opened her mouth to ask him to stay with her in the first place.

Ivy very much feared she was still somewhat enamored of him in spite of the pain of the past. He was here, and for a short time he could be hers again—and she desired it with every cell of her body.

He came inside and walked over to the bed. Then he reached for her shirt and tugged it up and over her head, tossing it aside. She wore nothing underneath, and cool air slipped over her skin.

"That's one of my old shirts, isn't it?" His voice was a low rumble that vibrated through her.

"Yes," she whispered. She'd slept in the thing for years now, rotating it with two others he'd left behind. They'd long since ceased to smell like him, but they were soft and huge on her. And she knew they were his even if they no longer carried his scent.

He palmed her bare breast and she gasped a little. "I can't begin to tell you how excited that makes me, knowing you've slept in my shirt for all these years. Did you ever touch yourself and think of me, Ivy?"

His thumb scraped over her nipple and she bit her lip. Her pussy was so wet that her juices would drip down her thighs at any minute. "Yes. All the time."

"I'd ask you to show me, but I think I'd be jealous of your fingers for getting to touch your sweet pussy."

"Then you touch me."

"Oh, I intend to." He lowered his head and took her swollen nipple between his lips.

Ivy threw her head back and moaned. "Dane—oh."

He sucked hard, tweaking her other nipple with his thumb and forefinger as he did so. Her legs trembled and her back arched as she tried to press her breast farther into his mouth.

He slid a hand down her belly, over her hip, and then skimmed the hairline of her pubic curls. She wanted him to touch her so badly it hurt.

He didn't at first, his fingers dancing lightly over her labia and then down her left thigh.

"So wet," he said against her nipple.

"You haven't even touched me yet. How do you

know?"

"I can feel your heat, Ivy. You're practically burning up with need."

This time, he slid his fingers into the seam of her sex. When he stroked across her clit, she nearly came undone. How could she be so excited when it had only been a couple of hours ago that they'd had sex in the alley?

"Do you have any idea how hard it makes me that you're this excited for me?"

"I hope you'll show me. Soon."

He laughed. "I will… but first I need to taste you, Ivy. Lie down and spread those pretty legs."

Ivy did as he said, lying back on the bed and opening her legs. Dane eased between them, putting his arms beneath her thighs and lifting her higher until his mouth hovered right over the place she wanted him to touch so badly.

"I've missed this," he said, and then he dropped his head and slid his tongue into her slit.

Ivy cried out. Her clit was swollen and aching, and when he traced his tongue around it, she thought she might come out of her skin.

"You're exactly like I remember. Velvety soft, sweet."

Ivy reached down and threaded her fingers through his hair. She arched her hips up to meet his mouth, riding against the smoothness of his tongue and the roughness of the stubble on his face.

The combination was enough to send her rocketing over the edge into a screaming orgasm that shook her with its power. When she came back to herself enough to open her eyes and look at him, he was watching her with one arched eyebrow.

"Good?"

"What do you think?"

"I think you need another to make sure."

"No, not yet," she gasped. She was still too sensitive, and she clutched at him as he dropped his head. But he didn't stop. He licked her mercilessly until her body caught fire again. It didn't take long. Soon she arched her back and cried for more—begged for more—until the pressure inside her crested and she came with a sharp, shuddering cry.

Sweat beaded on her skin, and her limbs were boneless. She lay on the bed, her body zinging with sparks, and thanked the heavens that she'd asked him to come to her room. Maybe it wasn't wise with their history, but considering the long drought in her sex life, it was the best idea she'd ever had.

Until morning, of course.

"Maybe I should take this slower, but that's not going to happen," Dane said, crawling up her body and positioning himself between her legs. "I need you too much, Ivy."

Then he plunged inside her and her body came alive once more.

EIGHTEEN

DANE IGNORED THE VOICE IN his head that told him this was probably not the best idea he'd ever had. Who could pay attention to a chiding voice when it felt so fucking fantastic not to?

Whatever the consequences, he'd pay them tomorrow.

He was buried inside his ex-wife, her taste still on his tongue, her legs wrapped around him, and he couldn't think of another damned thing except what it felt like to move his hips and pull out of her before slamming back inside her again.

She gasped, but he knew it wasn't from anything other than the deepest pleasure. He knew Ivy. Still knew her body better than he thought he would. Still knew what made her come unglued.

He fisted his hands in her hair and tilted her face up so he could kiss her. She met his mouth eagerly, her tongue rolling against his. He lifted his hips and plunged into her again and again.

Her pussy gripped him tight, her walls slick and hot

106

and wonderful. He loved being inside her, loved the way his balls tightened and tingled as he rocked into her.

He'd fucked other women since their divorce, but it hadn't felt like this. Why hadn't it felt like this?

Stop thinking, dude.

But he couldn't, not really. Oh, he could shove the thinking part of his brain to the back and enjoy the physical, but deep inside he wanted to know why it didn't feel this good with anyone else. Why it never had.

From the moment he'd seen Ivy in that bar over five years ago, nothing had ever been the same. He didn't believe in love at first sight, but he'd known he had to have her. And then he'd known he had to keep her.

Life didn't always work out the way you intended though.

Ivy arched and writhed beneath him, her body a beautiful instrument of pleasure.

He wanted it to last this time, and he was already dangerously close to coming.

He pulled out of her as she cried out, then urged her onto her hands and knees. She looked at him over her shoulder, and he thought he'd never seen anything more beautiful in his life—Ivy's sensual eyes watching him, her wet lips parted slightly, her naked skin gleaming in the moonlight streaming in the windows, and her glistening pussy beckoning him inside.

"Don't stop, Dane."

"I'm not stopping." He put his knees on the outside of hers and put her legs together. Then he positioned his cock and glided inside her welcoming body.

Like that, she was incredibly tight. She moaned and dropped her head to the pillow. Her fists gathered handfuls of the sheets.

"Is it too much?" he asked as sweat beaded on his forehead.

"Yes—no—oh, God."

Alarm rolled through him. "Ivy, am I hurting you?"

"Not like this, no."

When he hesitated, she reached around and cupped his balls. "Fuck me, Dane. I need you to fuck me."

He held her hips and plunged into her body again and again. He had no idea what it felt like for her, but if it was half as good as it was for him, it had to be pretty fucking incredible.

"Yes, oh yes," she cried as he pumped harder into her.

He reached around and stroked his index finger over her clit and she stiffened. Then she bucked against him and he knew she was about to explode.

He wanted to go with her. He let loose the tight rein he had on his control and stroked her harder even as he moved faster inside her. The walls of her pussy tightened, and the tingling in the base of his spine grew stronger.

And then he lost it. He shot himself deep inside her, his cock swelling even as her walls gripped him hard.

Ivy moaned his name as she came, her body stiffening for a long moment before going limp beneath him. He let her down easy, coming down on top of her, his cock still buried inside her.

She was breathing hard, and so was he. He shifted his weight so he wouldn't crush her into the mattress. Then he dipped his head to her shoulder and tasted the warmth of her skin and the saltiness of her sweat. His heart swelled with feelings he'd thought long buried. The intensity of it nearly choked him. He told himself it was only a temporary resurgence based on nostalgia and great sex. He didn't suddenly love this woman again. That was impossible.

"Regrets?" he asked her, because now that the heat of the moment was over, maybe she'd want him to go. And maybe he should go, quite honestly. Sex on a mission wasn't standard—then again, he'd never been on a mission with his ex-wife either.

"Lots," she breathed. "But this isn't one of them. You?"

"I regret that it's over and I can't do it again immediately."

She giggled, and his heart turned over at the sweet sound. "Losing your studliness, Dane? I remember when you used to come four or five times in a night."

He was still hard and he flexed his hips until she gasped. "Plenty of studliness, Ivy. I was talking about you. You said it had been a while, and I'm trying to be a gentleman and not make you too sore."

She turned her head and met his lips. He kissed her softly.

"I'll worry about that tomorrow. I've been sex-deprived for far too long to not take advantage of you while I can."

He withdrew from her body and rolled onto his back. She climbed on top of him and sank down on his cock. They both groaned.

"I like the way you take advantage of me," he said. "Feel free to use me up until I'm a shell of my former self."

She lifted her body and then lowered herself again, sinking farther down than before. He loved seeing his cock disappear inside her, loved watching her slick walls devour him.

"Hang on tight, Dane. I'm not going to be the only one who's sore tomorrow…"

NINETEEN

IT WAS BEFORE DAWN WHEN Dane bolted awake. He sat upright, listening hard in the darkness. Something woke him, but he didn't know what. Beside him, Ivy slept soundly, her naked form curled under the sheet, her hair fanning out over the pillow. His heart kicked in his chest at the sight of her. It was a familiar feeling, and a difficult one to process at the same time.

He reached for his gun on the night table and slipped from the bed. Then he crept through the bungalow, listening for noise.

A scraping sound came from the front door as if someone was trying to force the lock. A moment later, the door opened—but the chain stopped it from going any farther.

Dane's blood rushed inside his veins as adrenaline pumped through him. Someone—some *asshole*—had the nerve to break into his bungalow. It was unbelievable.

A cold fury rolled through him. He wasn't scared. Not even close. He was a military machine, ready to protect and defend his territory. He crept closer to the door, his gun held high, waiting for the bastard's next move.

It came when someone heaved their weight against the door in an attempt to dislodge the screws holding the security chain in the wall. Another shove and a grunt. There was a low curse—was it Spanish?—and then someone shoved again.

"Dane?"

Dane swore as he turned and saw Ivy silhouetted in the bedroom door. She'd slipped on a T-shirt and she stood there, swaying softly as if she were still half-asleep.

He crossed swiftly to her side and took her arm. Then he bent to her ear. "Go back in the bedroom, Ivy."

But she was more alert now, and she stiffened as she spied the light coming inside the partially opened front door.

"Is someone trying to break in?" she hissed.

"Yes. *Go.*"

She turned and went back into the bedroom, and he breathed a sigh of relief. But then she was back, her pistol at the ready, and his stomach fell.

"What the fuck?" he asked in a furious whisper.

Her eyes glittered. "What do you mean what the fuck? I'm as qualified as you," she whispered back.

"Hardly," he growled.

Outside, someone shouted—and whoever was at the door stopped trying to break it in. Dane swore as he sprinted for the door. He flattened himself against the wall and waited for a moment, but no one tried to come inside. Then he yanked off the chain and ripped the door open.

No one was there. He slipped down the walkway, sweeping his weapon wide. When he got to the end, he stopped and searched the empty pathways. The pink light of dawn was beginning to cut into the gloom of the thick foliage. Up ahead, someone moved down the path. He sprinted but drew up short when the figure turned and he came face-to-face with Ivy's partner.

Ace Martin looked pissed—but it was the gun pointed at Dane that made him pause. Then Ace cocked an eyebrow.

"Nature walking, SEAL man?"

"What the fuck are you talking about?"

Ace's gaze dropped. "The package, pretty boy. It's all dangling free. And I have to say that I'm mighty impressed."

Fuck. Dane hadn't thought about the fact he was naked when he'd slipped from bed.

"Did you see anyone?"

Ace frowned. "No, I'm just hanging out here for my health. Of course I saw someone, asshole. Two men, trying to break into your bungalow. When I made them, they ran. I couldn't fire because I didn't wanna risk hitting either of you inside."

"Why the fuck did you stop them? I could have neutralized them, and then we'd know who they're working for."

"Excuse me for trying to save your fine ass, but I saw dudes trying to break in and I reacted."

"Why were you near our bungalow so early anyway?"

Ace flourished a hand over his clothing. Shorts, an armband with his phone tucked inside, earbuds, and a moisture-wicking shirt. A runner. Figured.

"I was up anyway. Thought I'd check the perimeter."

"What's going on?"

Dane spun as Ivy came up behind him on the path.

She was still in the T-shirt, still holding her weapon, and his heart clenched at the sight of her looking so small and vulnerable in the early-morning light.

"You need to take cover, Ivy," Dane said. "It's dangerous for you to be here."

She cocked an eyebrow. "I'm not the one who's naked."

"Those men are long gone," Ace said, coming up beside him. "They weren't professionals. Probably petty thieves looking to rob guests."

"You can't really be that stupid," Dane said. "This is the second time someone has specifically targeted a bungalow where Ivy was staying. And then there's the threat on her answering machine."

Ace's eyes flashed. "Then why didn't they stay to complete the job? Why run away when I show up? They could have shot me and finished the job they'd come to do."

"Not if they're here for something more than a hit." Dane shook his head. "They haven't gone anywhere, except possibly back to their base of operations. They're waiting for the right moment to do what they came here to do."

He thought Ace would scoff, but the dude looked thoughtful. "You think they want to grab her?"

Dane didn't like that thought at all, but it was the one that made the most sense to him. "Yeah."

Ace's chest puffed out. "If what you say is right, Ivy can't stay here. She needs to be in protective custody."

Ivy drew herself up then, her expression hardening. "No. No way. We're here for a reason, Ace, and I intend to see that those bastards don't make it to the mainland. This is far more important than any threats to me."

Dane wanted to argue that point, but now wasn't the time.

"We aren't solving anything by standing here fighting about it," Dane said. "We need to keep searching."

"You're going to get arrested, hot stuff," Ace replied, his gaze sliding over Dane yet again. "People are waking up, and some little old lady is bound to take exception to the sight of your naked ass strolling through the resort. Take Ivy back to your bungalow and alert your team. If there's anything to find, they'll find it."

Dane hated that the dude made sense. "You're right. Ivy?"

Her chin was in the air. "Fine, yes, let's go."

She turned and started moving back down the path, but Ace called out one last time. "You're wearing the shirt your ex was wearing yesterday. Don't think I don't know what this means, naughty girl. Don't come crying to me when it all goes to shit, okay?"

Ivy flipped him the bird and kept walking. When they reached the bungalow, Dane did a quick check, then bolted the door behind them. The chain was still intact, but it was looser than before. Obviously, they couldn't stay here.

"You should get dressed," he said.

Ivy looked up at him with soft eyes that contained a hint of frustration and perhaps even fear. "Last night..." She dropped her gaze, and he knew he wasn't going to like whatever she said. "It can't happen again. It was... amazing—but we know how it's going to turn out."

He wanted to grab her, and he wanted to howl. He did neither. He'd expected this quite honestly. Because he knew her, and he knew she'd run. "So that's it, huh? I'm a one-night stand now?"

This time she met his gaze, her green eyes flashing fire. "What do you propose, Dane? A new relationship? I work for the DEA, and you're a SEAL. It could be months before we see each other again."

He knew she was right, and yet part of him wanted to tell her it didn't matter. That they'd figure it out. Because one thing he knew after a night with her was that he hadn't stopped being addicted. Not at all.

But what good was an addiction to someone when you couldn't make anything else work? He wasn't giving up his career for her. She wasn't giving up hers for him. They'd already risked enough by falling into bed together on a crucial operation. Best to put it behind them and move on.

"Whatever you want, Ivy," he said, turning away from her and strolling over to flip the coffeepot on.

He heard the door to the bathroom shut, and then he retrieved his phone to dial his team leader. Before he could press the first button, the phone buzzed.

"Erikson," he answered.

"We have intel on *Bad Medicine*," Matt said. "Need you to get over here ASAP."

TWENTY

IVY FELT LIKE HELL AS she looked at herself in the mirror. She didn't know why she'd told Dane they couldn't be together again, except that she'd looked at him standing there naked and ready to defend her, and her heart had thumped impossibly hard. Her stomach had squeezed tight, and feelings she'd thought she'd buried slid and writhed beneath the surface of her skin.

She was in danger of feeling too much, and she'd panicked. But it was the right choice, because she couldn't go through the anguish. She couldn't risk her heart again, knowing that she might not be enough for him. That he might get bored or fed up and leave her the way her father had.

Ivy lowered her head a moment and concentrated on breathing. She knew why her father had left. Her mother never said so, but Ivy knew it was *her* fault. A kid changed things, and he hadn't been ready for those changes. When Ivy's mother wanted to settle down in one place and raise her, give her some stability, her father wanted nothing of it. He'd used the Navy as his excuse, sailing away for months at a time. And then one day he left for good.

A rap sounded on the door and she jumped. "Yes?"

"We have to get over to Matt Girard's cabin. They've got intel on *Bad Medicine*."

"Be a few seconds," she said before hurriedly cleaning up and pulling on the silk tank and cropped pants she'd left hanging on the shower rod last night. When she emerged, Dane was dressed and waiting for her. He looked lethal in his cargo pants, deck shoes, and a white T-shirt that molded to his impressive pecs. She knew he had a gun tucked away in an ankle holster and a knife strapped to his belt. He was handsome and virile, and her belly fluttered anew at the thought of all they'd done to each other in the night.

He looked up at her as she walked into the room. His eyes were chilly.

"Grab your gear, Ivy. We aren't coming back here."

She hurried to the room they'd shared last night, pointedly ignoring the rumpled sheets as she grabbed everything and stuffed it into her suitcase. When she reached the door, she paused to look at the bed one more time.

It was one night of sex. One damn night—and already she felt as hooked on him as she ever had when she'd been his wife.

When she turned to go, Dane was watching her. She didn't speak, just stared back at him until he reached down and picked up his own bag, breaking the eye contact.

"Let's go," he told her.

They walked in silence to the cabin where HOT was meeting. It was still early, but there were tourists out now, walking the paths, going to the beach for sunrise views, getting an early breakfast, or hitting the gym. Some of those people looked happy, and Ivy envied them. What must it be like to be on a vacation with your lover, enjoying the amenities and having nothing more pressing to decide than whether to go to dinner or order room service because you were so into each other you couldn't bother getting dressed?

She wouldn't know. She'd never known because she'd never stopped panicking long enough to lose herself in the moment.

When they reached their destination, Dane opened the door and waited for her to go first. Several of the guys looked up when she walked in. She dropped her bag on the floor and kept on walking over to where someone had made a pot of coffee. She poured a cup, grabbed a donut from a tray, and took a seat beside Ace.

He gave her one of his concerned looks, but she shrugged it off and then patted his hand. He gave his head a slight shake, and she knew she was being chastised for sleeping with Dane. She deserved it considering how often she'd sworn to him that Dane had been a jerk.

Matt walked to the front of the room and started to speak. "We've had some intel that indicates *Bad Medicine* is going out today, but not for the usual fishing run. They aren't taking on passengers, and the crew is made up of the men we have in our dossiers. They're either making a practice run, or they've made contact with our sub."

"We need to be out there." It was Dane who'd spoken.

"Yes, we do. We've arranged to rent some fishing boats. We're going sailing today like a bunch of tourists."

"They can't possibly be planning to offload a missile in broad daylight," Chase Daniels said.

Fiddler, they called him. She wondered why. Did he play a fiddle? Or was it just a joke of some sort? She knew that call signs often were jokes or plays on the obvious. Dexter "Double Dee" Davidson—now that was obvious, though why they didn't just call him DeeDee and be done with it she didn't know. She understood Flash Gordon and Billy the Kid. Knight Rider for McKnight, Big Mac for MacDonald, Brandy for Brandon—wow, these guys weren't all that original, were they? Iceman was one of those dudes who seemed cool under pressure, so maybe that's where they'd gotten his name.

And she had no idea what Matt's name was, come to think of it. Dane was Viking, which made sense considering his real name was so Norse sounding.

"No, probably not," Matt said. "But they could be planning to get into position and troll the area all day. The sub will probably surface sometime after nightfall." His gaze slewed over to Ivy and Ace. "You two will have to sit this one out. You aren't trained for this kind of op."

Cold anger fizzed inside Ivy's veins. "We damn sure are. Who do you think confiscates drugs coming into the US? The Junior League of Key West? We've worked with the Coast Guard to apprehend smugglers. This isn't our first dance, you know."

"It's dangerous out there," Dane said.

Ivy swung around to glare at him. "You think I don't know that? What part of 'we've done this before' don't you get?"

She could see Ace grinning beside her, and she wanted to smack him. He was enjoying this far too much when he should be as incensed as she was.

"They can play tourists," Big Mac said, shrugging.

"Put them on a cabin cruiser and put Ivy in a bikini. It's not like we haven't infiltrated a secure compound before by using a woman in a bikini as a distraction."

"And what a fine distraction your wife was," Chase said. "Especially when she took off her top."

"Watch it, asshole," Big Mac growled. "Lucky's not here to save your ass if I decide to kick it for you."

Chase kept on grinning. "I'll tell Lucky. You know she hates it when you get all macho about her role on the team."

"Son of a bitch," Big Mac muttered, but he didn't take a swing at Chase.

Ivy thought she might like to meet this Lucky. She sounded like a hell of a woman if she could make that big man back down with only the threat of her learning he'd kicked someone's ass on her behalf.

"It's not a bad idea," Matt said. "Worked the last time, didn't it? Fine, Ivy and Ace can go on the cabin cruiser."

"She's not wearing a bikini," Dane said to the room.

Ivy stood and popped her hands on her hips as she faced her ex-husband. "Stay out of this, Dane. I'll wear my fucking birthday suit if it helps get those assholes before they can deploy their weapon."

Dane looked militant. "You don't need to be out there. Stay here and monitor the marina with Ace—"

"Fuck you," Ivy shot back. She was aware the gazes of the men were bouncing between her and Dane like a Ping-Pong ball. No doubt they were highly entertained, but she was furious that Dane would try to shove her to the sidelines.

"Enough," Matt barked. "Ivy and Ace can help. Tourists on the cabin cruiser, observation only. We can always use extra eyes on the perimeter. Wear a bikini or not, I don't really fucking care. Now, can we get back to business, or do you two want to discuss wardrobe issues some more?"

TWENTY-ONE

IT WAS A GLORIOUS DAY in the Keys, sunny and breezy, not too hot yet, with a sky so blue it hurt the eyes and a sparkling ocean spreading as far as a person could see. In the end, Ivy and Ace wound up on the cabin cruiser alone while the team split themselves between fishing boats. They were in the area, but not always visible. Occasionally she lifted the binoculars and spotted one of them, but she didn't know which one.

Bad Medicine had left the dock on Emerald Key earlier, but there was no sign of her out here. Ivy adjusted her bikini top—she'd worn the bikini, but she'd knotted a floor-length wrap over the bottoms—and lifted the binoculars again.

She thought of that moment when she'd walked onto the dock and Dane had seen her. His eyes ate her up, but then his jaw hardened and he turned away, pretending not to care. She knew it was pretense because she knew Dane. He cared—and she'd been both gratified that he did and angry with herself at the same time. Angry because she couldn't stop reacting to him, angry because last night had felt so damn good. Angry because she'd told him no more.

She loved the possessive look in his eyes even when she pushed him away. And that was wrong of her. She shouldn't regret doing the right thing for them both, and yet there was a pit in her stomach that hadn't stopped aching.

She scanned the horizon again. The radio had been silent for over an hour. They had a secure channel, but there was no chatter at the moment. Ace kicked back on the deck, cell phone in one hand, icy cold drink in the other. The scent of sun-warmed coconut wafted from him.

"Man, this is the life, Ivy. Think we could get stationed down here permanently?"

Ivy lowered the binoculars and looked at him. He was naked except for a tiny Speedo. He was also gleaming with oil. She couldn't help but smile.

"I doubt that. Besides, what would you do about Maximo?"

Ace's face grew dreamy. "I'd ask him to move down here with me."

"Isn't that a little fast? You've only been dating for a couple of months."

Ace gave her a look. "Seriously? You're going to give me advice when you fucked your ex-husband last night after swearing you never wanted to lay eyes on the bastard again?"

Ivy's cheeks burned. "You have no idea what happened, so stop trying to pry it out of me. Besides, we're talking about you."

Ace snorted, ignoring the second part of that statement and attacking the first. "Honey, that man is a walking orgasm waiting to happen—and he was naked and you were wearing his shirt this morning. You fucked him—and I really don't blame you, by the way. I'd fuck him too if he'd have me."

Ivy flopped down on the bench seat cushion. The boat rocked gently in the water and the radio played Top 40 hits. What was the point in denying it? Ace was her partner and probably her best friend.

"Fine, I had a lapse in judgment. I haven't had sex in too long to remember, and I know how amazing it can be with Dane. So yes, when he kissed me, I lost all my good intentions. And the orgasms were completely worth it. I don't regret it at all."

Which wasn't completely true, but Ace didn't need to know that.

Ace's brow wrinkled. "So what happens when this is over? You seeing him again?"

Ivy lowered her head until her hair fell over her cheek, curtaining her face from his view. "I don't think it's a good idea… so no."

"Probably right then. The heart knows." Ace's phone dinged and he lifted it to peer at the text. Then he laughed. "Max sent me a dick pic. Want to see?"

Ivy held up a hand. "God no. What makes men think women want to see dicks on their phones?"

"I don't know about women, but I want to see as many as possible." His fingers flew over his screen.

Ivy pushed her hair behind her ear and turned her head to look at the water. It was peaceful out here, but she wasn't feeling very peaceful inside. No, she was feeling jumpy and achy. She was a bit sore, and that only made her think of Dane and what he'd done to her last night.

And what she'd done to him. No, she didn't want a

dick pic—but she wouldn't mind seeing his dick again up close and personal.

Which was precisely why she couldn't. Ivy frowned. Dammit, one night of bliss was going to cost her heavily when she couldn't stop thinking about Dane for the next few weeks. Months.

Years.

No, not years. No way.

Except, dammit, from the first moment she'd met Dane, she hadn't known how to shake him from her system. She hadn't wanted to in the early days, and then when she had, it just wasn't happening. She'd eventually gotten to the point where whole days would pass and she wouldn't think about him, but that had taken time.

That had been busted all to hell the minute she walked into HOT HQ and saw him standing there, staring back at her like a forgotten wet dream.

Something bounced on the horizon, and Ivy looked through the binoculars again. It was a speedboat, but not one she recognized. The boat hopped over the waves toward them. It was a big ocean, and they'd seen boat traffic on and off for the past couple of hours—but something about the purposeful way this one moved toward them felt different from the other boats they'd seen.

Ace swore softly. Then he sat up to watch the approaching craft. "Is that one of ours?"

"Doesn't look like it. Besides, wouldn't they hail us on the radio?"

"Maybe they needed to go silent."

Even as he said it, Ivy's neck prickled in warning. The boat was growing bigger now, and it wasn't changing course. It was probably nothing… but her blood iced over and her belly flipped. She reached into the beach bag where she'd packed her weapon and withdrew it.

"I don't like this," she said. "Something's wrong."

Ace glanced at his phone one last time. His face went white for a second before he swore and tossed it aside. "Agreed. Let's get the fuck out of here."

He grabbed his weapon from the floor where he'd laid it and jumped up to start the boat.

"Pull the anchor," he told her, and Ivy rocketed into gear.

The windlass had a hand crank, and she began to turn it as quickly as she could manage. Maybe they were over-reacting, but it was easier to dial back their response after they'd put distance between themselves and the approaching boat than to ramp it up too late.

Ivy's muscles screamed as she turned the crank and the anchor came slowly up from the bottom. At least it wasn't deep here, so the anchor wasn't out too far, but it still took time.

When the anchor was in and the engine purred, Ace rolled the stick back and the boat slid forward.

"We'll take it nice and slow," he said. "Make it look like we're out for a casual sail."

Ivy picked up the radio and called in. "Shark Three on the move. Unwanted guests headed our way."

The radio crackled and Dane's voice snapped back at her. "Friendlies?"

"Not sure. They're coming fast and not deviating."

The speedboat shot through the water, heading straight for them now. It could be joyriders, sure. Kids out for a good time. But every instinct she had told her it wasn't. The approach was too purposeful, too swift.

She scanned the boat again with the binoculars. Three men stood in the bow, bouncing with the waves. They wore sunglasses, and their hair whipped in the wind. One of them drove. The other pointed toward them.

And the third held a rifle, which he brought to his shoulder in one smooth move.

"Go," she screamed.

Ace gunned their boat and she fell to her knees. Ivy never heard a sound—but a moment later Ace slumped over the console and slid sideways in slow motion, a jagged red stain following him down to the floor.

TWENTY-TWO

SHARK TWO ROCKETED TOWARD IVY and Ace's position. Dane scanned the horizon with binoculars, looking for something—anything.

"We'll get there," Chase called over the rush of wind.

Dane merely nodded. When they spotted the cabin cruiser, Knight Rider gave the fishing boat more gas and they leapt forward in the water. He throttled back in order to glide into the cruiser's space without ramming into her or sending her rocking too hard. There was no one at the helm, and Dane toed a hold on the side of the fishing boat, rope in hand, waiting until the moment he could leap onto the other craft.

When they were close enough, he jumped. There was no sign of Ivy up top, but Ace lay on the floor in a pool of blood and Dane rushed to him. The man's eyes fluttered open as Dane pressed his fingers against the belly wound to stop the blood flow.

Garrett "Iceman" Spencer was beside him in two seconds, ripping into a med kit and taking out field dressings and strong painkillers.

"No one below," he said as he started to tend to Ace. He cleaned the wound as best as he could, dropped a clotting agent on it, and packed it with gauze while Dane shot morphine into Ace's veins.

Dane could hear Chase calling in and informing mission control what they'd found. Ace, but no Ivy. Goddamn, where was she?

They had no choice but to get Ace back to shore as fast as possible, and that was going to entail calling a helicopter.

"Ivy," Ace choked out, his voice thin. "They took Ivy."

"Easy," Dane said, his heart thundering. Because he'd been considering the possibility they'd shot her. That maybe she'd fallen overboard and drowned, or died from a gunshot wound. That they'd be trolling for her lifeless body and he'd be wondering how he'd hold it together when they found her.

Ace gripped his arm with surprisingly strong fingers for a man who'd been shot. "Afraid... My fault."

"What? What do you mean it's your fault?"

"Dude," Iceman said, wrapping a hand around Dane's wrist. "Careful."

Dane realized he was squeezing Ace's arm and let go. But he wanted to shake the man and make him spill. His fault what?

"Phone."

Dane wasn't sure what the man was talking about, but he looked around the deck for a phone, found it lying on a cushion. It was wet, but not submerged in water. Dane dried it off and slid the bar.

"Code," he barked.

"Four, five… nine, eight."

Dane punched it in and Ace's phone opened to him. "What am I looking for?"

"Max…," he wheezed. "Messages."

Dane brought up the messages and clicked on Max. There was a dick pic, which he did not appreciate in the least, but it was the conversation that chilled him. Mostly it was normal, flirtatious. But the last comment was the one that changed the tone.

I'm sorry. I had no choice.

Shit. "We need to get someone to pick this guy up."

Ice settled in Dane's gut. He found Max's contact information in the phone and gave it to Chase, who radioed it in.

"Chopper's on the way," Chase said. "Team heading out to collect Max."

Dane wanted to snarl. "What about the boat these bastards were in? It can't be gone. It's only been a few minutes."

"Shark Four is in pursuit of a craft, but it's too fast."

"We'll lose her," Dane said, frustration and fear bubbling inside him.

"We won't let that happen," Iceman replied. "No fucking way. We'll get her back."

Dane looked up at the sky as if he could make the chopper come faster. But the sky was silent… and time was running out.

"Where is my submarine, Miss McGill?"

Ivy's head pounded and her mouth was dry. She heard the voice, but she couldn't seem to open her eyes to look at whoever was speaking. She tried to shift her body from its cramped position, realized she was lying on a hard surface. Her cheek was cool where it touched wood.

And then water splashed down over her head and she sputtered. She accidentally breathed some in and she coughed violently. Her lungs ached and her throat burned. Somehow she managed to push herself up against the wall until she was half sitting, half lying.

She cracked an eye open and peered into the room. It was dark other than a beam of light coming from a point in front of her. The light shone on her, and she blinked to stop the stab of pain in her eyes.

Where was she? And—oh my God, Ace! She scrambled up a little higher, her chest aching as she dragged in air. The last thing she remembered was Ace slumping on the console—she'd scrambled to her feet from where she'd been knocked down, but the boat had hit another wave before she could get to the console and she'd fallen against something and hit her head.

Now she was here.

"My submarine, Miss McGill. Where is it?"

Ivy licked her lips and tried to focus on the man who'd spoken. The room she was in was big and bare, with only a chair and a table and a light. A warehouse of some kind, confirmed by the smell of oil and fish.

And then her gaze landed on the man. A slick man in an expensive suit. Tall, black hair, slightly balding. She recognized that face...

Miguel Ruiz. Oh holy shit.

"Where is my partner?"

"Do you mean Mr. Martin? Unfortunately, I do not know. He is not the one I'm interested in at the moment." He bent down and grasped her chin. His grip was not kind. "You cost me a lot of money, Miss McGill. I am not a happy man. If you give me back my submarine, I may let you live."

His fingers softened a bit—and then they trailed down her bare flesh, between the exposed rounds of her breasts in the bikini top, and her skin crawled. Her gag reflex was strong at the moment, but she wouldn't let him see it. It would only anger him.

"I don't have your submarine, Señor. The men you tried to negotiate with have it."

"You are as pretty as your mother was. Maybe even prettier."

Shock flooded Ivy. "You knew my mother?"

Miguel Ruiz laughed. "Knew her? So Maya never told you."

Ivy's heart skipped. A chill rolled down her spine. "Never told me what?"

Ruiz straightened and turned away, walking back to the chair he'd been sitting in and sinking down again. He crossed his legs one over the other and picked up a slim cigarillo from the metal table. Then he lit it and blew out a column of smoke.

"All this time you've spent trying to take down my network. Trying to end my business as if you have the right. And you had no idea."

"I know my mother died because of you. I know she thought she had nowhere to turn when my father abandoned her. You used her. Your people used her—and she died."

Razor blades sliced Ivy's throat as she spoke. Her voice was almost a hiss.

"Did you not ever wonder how your mother knew to come to the Ruizes in the first place?"

"She was Colombian. Her family probably worked for you or knew someone who did."

He laughed. "Oh yes, her family. *My* family, Miss McGill."

He took a drag on the cigarillo while her mind whirled. Was he saying…? She shook her head. *No.* No, she would have known. Someone would have told her. Granny? Did Granny know?

Oh, God.

"I see you are shocked. My little sister ran away with an American sailor when she was only eighteen. She was back ten years later, begging to return to the fold. I gave her one task to do. One simple task…"

"Simple? Swallowing sealed condoms full of drugs isn't simple! And it isn't safe. Did you even care when one of the condoms burst and killed her?"

He shrugged. "These things happen."

Ivy choked. He'd made his own sister run drugs? As a way to punish her for leaving home in the first place? God, he was sick! If she could get her hands around his neck, she'd squeeze until there was nothing left.

"You're disgusting. You don't care about anything but pouring more of your poison onto the streets, addicting more innocent people—"

"Innocent? You make it sound like they don't have a choice. But they do, Ivy. They all have a choice, and yet they snort or smoke or shoot up anyway. If I weren't fulfilling their need for escape with my product, someone else would. So why not me? No," he said, shaking his head, "you are a naïve girl—and a stupid one. Now tell me where to find my submarine before I get angry."

Ivy wanted to cry. And scream. This man had killed her mother. This man—this horrible, horrible man—was her *uncle*. It was unfathomable. And disgusting. How could she be connected to someone like him?

She felt betrayed, sick. And furious. Rage boiled hot in her belly, her blood. She wanted to kill this man, and yet she was the one at his mercy. Something inside her snapped. It was a risk, a huge risk, but she was going to take it.

"I don't know where your sub is," she spat. "But I know where it might be sometime tonight. I can take you there."

TWENTY-THREE

"THEY WERE TRACKING AGENT MCGILL by her phone," Colonel Mendez said.

Dane stood as still as a rock and watched the colonel talking on the sat-link video call.

"Agent Martin's boyfriend was working for Miguel Ruiz, and he planted GPS-tracking programs in both their phones. It's subtle technology, undetectable through normal means. They wouldn't have known anything was wrong."

"Can we track her with it?" Dane asked.

"We've got the frequency, so technically yes. But nothing's coming up yet. It's possible they've turned off her phone or taken her somewhere that's shielded. If she comes on the grid again, we'll find her."

Dane wanted to howl. That was the problem. She might not come on the grid at all, and Mendez knew it as well as they all did. For one thing, Miguel Ruiz wouldn't let her keep her phone once he had her. He might also end her life and dump her in the ocean for the sharks to eat before HOT could do a damn thing about it. And then what?

There was a hollow spot in Dane's chest that said he might lose his mind if that happened. He wasn't supposed to care so much—but he did. Goddamn, he did.

Chase put a hand on his shoulder and squeezed. "If they'd wanted her dead," he murmured, "they'd have killed her when they shot Ace. There's something else going on, and they need her for it."

Dane looked at the guys gathered round. They weren't his SEAL team, the guys he was used to working with—but they were every bit as good. They were thorough, professional, and the kind of warriors he was happy to have at his back. Hell, he was happy to be a part of them —and that surprised him in ways he hadn't thought about.

They were in the Army and he was in the Navy—but they were able to do things he hadn't considered as a SEAL, like take on missions such as this one with a freedom that he still hadn't wrapped his head around.

After the attack on Ace and Ivy, they'd had to regroup. *Bad Medicine* was still out, but they hadn't made contact with the sub. HOT had gathered on a single boat now that the sun was going down. This one was bigger and faster than the fishing boats they'd had before and was designed to attack swiftly and quietly.

He knew the tangos were still the priority, but damn if it wasn't killing him not to know where Ivy was. In spite of the excitement of this mission, the state-of-the-art equipment, he wanted to bail. He wanted to go after Ivy and let these guys deal with the Freedom Force.

But that wasn't happening because he had nowhere to go. *Fuck.*

"Agent Martin is out of surgery," the colonel continued. "He'll make it, though it'll probably be a long recovery. He'll be on desk duty for quite some time." Mendez looked away from the screen for a minute and then nodded to someone before turning back to face them. "Agent McGill's phone is transmitting again—moving east southeast in a line toward where she was taken."

"We have to intercept them," Dane said, his heart hammering.

Colonel Mendez's expression didn't change. "No need, son. They're coming straight for you."

"Uh, sir... do we have time to wait?" Matt asked.

Dane's chest tightened, but he knew why the question had to be asked. It was the kind of question he'd have asked if he was leading this team and Ivy wasn't his girl. *His girl.*

Mendez's mouth curved into a grin. Dane hadn't known the man for very long, but he knew enough to realize the colonel wasn't much of a smiler. That was encouraging. Wasn't it?

"A little bit of time, yes. Oh, and Viking?"

Dane hadn't looked away from the screen for even a second. "Yes, sir?"

"Got a surprise for you. Your SEAL team is on the way. ETA in about twenty minutes. You boys get Agent McGill—and then meet the SEALs and go get that fucking sub for the sake of every human being on this planet."

Ivy was handcuffed to the railing of the thirty-foot yacht. Miguel Ruiz stood at the helm along with another man. Six more men sat in the stern, holding rifles across their laps. Ivy bit the inside of her lip and tried to calm her racing heart.

She'd fed Ruiz a load of bullshit about the submarine surfacing tonight when she really didn't know if that was the case or not. All she knew was that she needed to get back to the zone and hope that HOT was still there. If they weren't, she didn't know what she would do.

Plan B, whatever that was.

Ruiz flipped her phone in his hand. She'd given him the access code because she'd had no choice. There was nothing in there for him other than a few phone numbers to DEA headquarters. Her boss's number was there. Ace's. A few other agents, but nothing critical. Some numbers were committed to memory, like the number she needed for her contacts at the CIA and the FBI. Not that those contacts usually did her much good considering the intel services didn't work well together. But it was something she'd cultivated, and something she kept tucked away for the future.

Future. Assuming she had one after tonight.

"It's really too bad you don't want to work for us," Ruiz said, turning to her as the yacht rode the waves. "You could have gone far in this business. Maybe taken over someday."

The thought made her want to retch. "Not interested in peddling death to kids."

He snorted a laugh. "So self-righteous. Maya was too, until she needed us again."

She hated hearing him mention her mother with such familiarity. She was still reeling from the knowledge that her mother was a Ruiz—that *she* was a Ruiz.

"She had no choice."

His dark eyes glittered. "Is that what you think? That she had no choice? That she couldn't have kept working doing something—anything—else? No, Maya returned because she was tired of working hard. She remembered the wealth and the prestige of being a Ruiz. She wanted it again, and she wanted you to grow up with those privileges instead of living on food stamps and wearing cheap clothing from secondhand stores."

Ivy's heart hurt. She'd been eight when her mother died, and she remembered complaining bitterly that her clothes weren't as nice as her friends' clothes. But was that enough to send her mother crawling back to a dangerous lifestyle?

"You didn't have to force her to smuggle. You chose to do that, not me, so stop trying to blame me for what happened to her."

He laughed. "You are guilty and you know it. But don't worry. After tonight you won't have to feel guilty ever again."

"You said you might let me live if you got your sub back."

"I said *might*. I'm undecided."

She knew the bastard was completely decided and had been from the first. He intended for her to die. Family ties didn't mean jack to this asshole. They didn't mean jack to her either in this case. If she could forget she and Miguel Ruiz shared the same DNA, she'd be a happy woman.

"You still don't have your sub. If you plan to kill me anyway, maybe I won't tell you where to look. If we're off by even a mile, you won't get it back."

"Yes, but getting my sub could mean the difference between a quick and painless death or something a bit more creative."

Ivy stared at him, refusing to look away even though she knew he wanted her to. But she hated the bastard, and if this was her last night on earth, she wasn't going down cowering.

He laughed—and then he slapped her so hard her cheek cracked against the Bimini support. The blow stung and she tasted blood. A reckless part of her wanted to glare at him again, but she very wisely kept her head turned and stared at the water. The sun was setting, and the sky blazed pink and purple to the west and black to the east. The water turned indigo.

Was it really only last night that she'd lain in Dane's arms and felt as if her world was right somehow, even though it terrified her? And was it really only this morning that she'd told him there could be nothing more between them? That one night of passion was all she had time for?

God, she felt like such a fool. She hadn't stopped feeling a damn thing for him. Now that she might not ever see him again, she knew how deluded she'd been. She still loved the big, bad, intense man who'd stolen her heart in a bar one night. Since the moment he'd walked over and asked her to dance, she'd been his.

Nothing had changed—and everything had. They weren't the same people they used to be—but he was the only one who made her feel like letting go. She'd resisted that feeling for so long, been terrified that if she let go, she'd fall. But Dane would be there to catch her. She knew that now.

Too late.

It was full dark by the time the boat reached the coordinates where Ruiz's men had shot Ace and captured her. *Oh, Ace.* Dear God, she hoped like hell he'd survived, but she doubted he had. He'd fallen, and there'd been so much blood. He hadn't moved at all before she'd been knocked out.

"Where is my sub?"

She was getting tired of the broken record. "We have to wait."

Ruiz's jaw was a hard line. "You had better not be lying to me, girl."

Ivy lifted her chin. Please let HOT still be here. Please let them be patrolling the waters and let them come investigating.

"I'm not. They're supposed to meet their contact at midnight one nautical mile to the east. If we move closer now, we could spook them. We have to stay here."

Ruiz moved toward her, and she cringed before she could stop herself. But all he did was uncuff her from the support and then cuff her wrists together in front of her body.

"We're going below," he told the man at the helm. "Notify me when there's something to report."

Ruiz grabbed her by the arm and shoved her down the stairs. Her feet caught in the wrap she'd tied around her waist so many hours ago and she fell to the bottom. Ruiz was on her in seconds, dragging her up and throwing her down again on the nearest cushioned surface.

It was only when he jerked the wrap from her body that she began to understand his purpose. Horror clawed its way into her throat. He was her uncle. *Her uncle!*

"Don't look so surprised," he told her as he shrugged out of his shirt. "You're a beautiful girl… and I'm a man who appreciates beauty…"

TWENTY-FOUR

DANE LOWERED THE BINOCULARS, HIS body as tense as a cat getting ready to pounce. They'd found the intruder's boat precisely where Mendez had said they would. Knight Rider powered in as close as he dared. They were running with lights out, but they weren't blind. This is what SEALs did. What HOT did. Dane loved the thrill of it, even if he was far too invested in this particular aspect of the op to enjoy it as much as he usually did.

"Looks like six armed men in the stern. One at the helm. No sign of Ivy."

"She could be stowed away down below," Iceman said.

"Can you pinpoint where her phone is transmitting from?" Matt asked Billy.

Kid tapped on his laptop. "Hard to pin down with one hundred percent accuracy, but I'd say it's coming from beneath the waterline."

Dane's insides churned. "So either she's down there, or someone with her phone is."

"Yep, that's the way I see it," Big Mac said. He

turned to Brandy and Double Dee, the sniper and spotter. "Think you guys can pop those assholes quick and clean?"

Brandy snorted. "You're fucking kidding, right?"

Big Mac grinned. "Just yanking your chain, dude."

"Let's get closer," Matt said. "We have no idea how many are below, so we need to be able to storm the boat as quickly as we can."

Chase throttled the boat into gear, and they glided softly through the water. The engines were quiet, a special prototype courtesy of DARPA. Dane would like to get his hands on something like that for his SEALs. It crossed his mind that if he stayed with HOT, that might just be a possibility.

They moved as close as they could without alerting the other craft—and then Brandy and Double Dee went to work. The bodies dropped before the report rang out on the night air. One, two, three, four, five, six, seven.

The men didn't have a chance to realize what was happening before they fell. Chase knocked the throttle into high gear, and they made for the yacht. When they came alongside, he'd already powered down enough to allow Dane and the guys to jump from one boat to the other.

Dane landed on the deck amidst bodies and tore for the cabin. But when he ripped the door open, gun up and ready to fire, a man stood in the center of the floor, his arm around Ivy's neck and a gun against her temple.

Relief didn't even have a chance to make its way through his system before rage arrived. Ivy was clothed only in a turquoise bikini. The top was perilously close to revealing her breasts, the cups shifted sideways and slipping as she held on to the arm of the man holding her and tried not to choke.

There were red marks on her abdomen, an angry slash from her belly to the top of her bikini bottoms. Finger marks. Dane saw red.

"Drop the gun or I'll kill her," the man said.

"And then you'll kill me. No."

The dude blinked. "You want me to shoot her?"

"No, but neither do you. She's your leverage. Drop her and I'm dropping you."

Ivy's green eyes were huge in her face, but he knew she understood what he was doing. He couldn't afford to feel fear right now. Couldn't afford tenderness or mercy. If he let those things out, if he let the very real fear he had for her safety show, it would mean the end of her life. And possibly his.

He gripped his MK45 tighter and kept it trained on the man's head. He could take the shot. He could drop the guy here and now—but the boat rocked hard in the water from the wake of the assault boat. If he was off by even a hair, he risked hitting Ivy.

And there would be no coming back from that.

"I'm a rich man. I could make it worth your while— worth your team's while—to let me leave here."

Dane pretended to consider it. "How much we talking?"

"One million."

"You said that so quickly I'm sure you can do better. Five million."

He'd figured out by now that this man was a Ruiz. He didn't know which one, but it didn't much matter. He was a dead man regardless of which scumbag Ruiz brother he was.

"Five million then. Call your team off and let me

leave in the boat. Once I'm safe in port, I'll let her go and you'll get your money."

Dane didn't have to look over his shoulder to know at least one of his HOT teammates was behind him, listening to everything this man said.

"What do you think? Sound fair?"

It was Ryan "Flash" Gordon's voice that filtered down to him. "Naw, not quite. There are nine of us—ten if you count Ivy. I think we need a million each."

"There you go," Dane said, surprised at how cool he managed to sound. "Ten mil. You get to walk away. But Ivy stays here and one of us goes with you. To make sure you make that transfer, of course."

Ruiz looked about as happy as an alligator in a purse factory. He was growing frustrated with the runaround, and his grip on Ivy had loosened. Not by much, but enough that she was no longer struggling to breathe.

The look in her eyes was pure fury as she stared at Dane over Ruiz's arm. He didn't know what that meant, but he was in the zone and unable to worry about it.

Please, God, just let him get her free. After that, he didn't care what happened.

Suddenly, Ivy rocketed into motion. Dane hadn't seen it coming, but she somehow managed to drop and spin, jerking herself loose from Ruiz's grip as she did so. It happened so fast that her captor lost his grip on his pistol, which clattered to the floor. It went off with a boom, and Dane screamed at Ivy.

But Ivy wasn't stopping. She sprang up off her feet, the heel of one hand aimed at Ruiz's face, the other holding her wrist for leverage. She rammed her palm into his nose—and he fell over backward, blood spewing from his face as he hit the floor with a thud.

Dane was at Ivy's side in one step, grabbing her and shoving her behind him as he aimed the pistol at Ruiz's head. But Ruiz wasn't moving.

"Did I kill him?"

Dane dropped and put his fingers against Ruiz's pulse. It throbbed beneath his fingers, but the man was out cold.

"He's alive."

"Fuck."

"Everything under control down there?" Flash peeked into the cabin.

Dane turned and nodded. "Yeah. Give us a sec."

He patted Ruiz down until he found the key to the handcuffs Ivy wore. Dane stood and unlocked them, then took the metal bracelets and wrapped them around Ruiz's wrists. Tight.

When he turned again, Ivy was standing there rubbing her wrists. She'd straightened her bikini top, but blood spattered the fabric and her smooth skin.

Ruiz's blood. Dane sucked in a breath and felt the beginnings of a tremor roll through him. He could have lost her. Forever.

She looked up at him then, her eyes uncertain in her pretty face. He didn't know what was going on behind those eyes, but he couldn't stop himself from dragging her against his body and burying his face in her hair.

"Ivy… Shit, that was stupid."

TWENTY-FIVE

IVY STIFFENED IN DANE'S ARMS. He was warm and big, and she felt safe tucked up against him—but then he had to go and say something like that. She pushed herself away from his big body and glared up at him.

He was dressed for combat, his face painted and his hair hidden beneath a black balaclava. He was also bristling with weaponry. His black assault suit had pockets and loops, and there was more equipment on him than she could count.

He was, in short, scary-looking.

But she wasn't afraid of him. She was pissed.

"Damn you," she growled. "I just took that asshole down, and you want to critique my decision-making skills? I got tired of waiting for you to shoot his ass."

Dane's blue eyes shone from his darkened face. "Shoot him? We're on a rolling boat and he had a gun to your head. How the fuck was I supposed to shoot him when you were in danger?"

"It's your job, mister. I expect it's not the first time you've shot a target while standing on a bobbing deck."

She could see his Adam's apple move. "No... but it's the first time some piece of shit had a gun to the head of someone I care about."

Care about. Her heart thumped. He cared... well, hell, she knew that, didn't she? But did he still love her? Could he ever love her again? She wanted desperately to know, but now wasn't the time to ask.

She reached up and put her hand to his cheek. Then she smiled. Adrenaline tumbled through her system, and she hadn't quite gotten it under control yet. Hell, she might fall apart at any minute. But for the moment, this was what she wanted to do.

"It's okay, Dane. I'm fine." Her smile faded. "Did... did you find Ace?"

"He's in the hospital. He's going to make it."

Ivy's bottom lip quivered. Now that was just the news she needed to make her lose it. A tear rolled down her cheek, and then another. "Thank God. Oh, thank God."

"Yeah."

Two of the guys came down the stairs to collect Ruiz. They looked every bit as big and bad as Dane did, and she thanked God for them as well. They'd been here, and they'd come for her when they had a mission that was far more important than a single life.

"What about the sub? Did you find it?"

"That's the next stop," Dane said. "They're surfacing somewhere near Pineapple Key in about twenty-five minutes. We'll be waiting."

"Then we should probably go and get them."

He let his gaze drop over her body. "You're cold."

Goose bumps started to prickle on her skin like ants heading for a party. "A little."

He slung his arm around her and guided her up the stairs. The bodies of Ruiz's men slumped in the stern. She didn't much care. She stepped past them all and went over to the side where the commando boat was moored. Dane handed her up, and then someone on the other side helped her over.

Dane was beside her quickly, and he grabbed a blanket from somewhere and wrapped it around her. She took it gratefully, not only because she was cold, but because she felt exposed in this stupid bikini. Not that the men were staring at her, because they weren't. They very deliberately were not, she thought.

"Hey," Chase, aka Fiddler, said, and she looked up. "You okay?"

"Perfectly fine."

One of the others grinned. Iceman. "You did a number on that man's face. Nice work."

"You saw that?"

"Not exactly, but it couldn't have been Viking. He was too busy trying not to shit his pants because the dude had you in a choke hold."

A couple of the other guys snorted.

"Hey, let some asshole take your girl hostage and see how you feel," Dane retorted.

Iceman's expression sobered. "Already been there, man. I feel you, believe me."

Ivy was still reeling about being called Dane's girl when the boat started to slide through the water. She watched Ruiz's yacht recede in the distance.

"The Coast Guard will retrieve it," Dane said at her side, and she glanced up at him. His presence made her heart skip even when she didn't want it to. There was so

151

much she wanted to say to him—but not here on the deck of an assault boat filled with military commandos.

Of which he was one. She studied him for a moment, her heart filling with pride. Dane had always been meant for great things, though being a SEAL wasn't quite what she'd envisioned. She'd thought he would join the Navy and learn to command a ship. She'd never pictured this.

It suited him. She reached for his hand. He didn't shrink away. He twined his fingers in hers and squeezed.

"Don't you do anything stupid tonight, Dane," she said as they moved toward Pineapple Key. "I want to talk to you when this is all over."

He pressed her fingers to his lips and a shiver ran down her spine. "I want to do more than talk… but we can start with that."

When the boat slowed, Ivy didn't think anything of it. But then another boat was there, coming alongside, and her chest squeezed tighter than a drum. She recognized the Coast Guard trawler. Instead of waiting for it, they'd gone to meet it.

She knew what it meant that the boat was here and they were slowing.

"You aren't leaving me," she said fiercely, squeezing hard on Dane's hand.

He threaded his fingers through her hair and pulled her in close. "Not my choice, Ivy—but you'll be safer this way. You don't need to be in the middle of this op. You were never meant to be anyway."

"Dane, goddammit, if anything happens to you—"

He smiled, and she felt the power of it all the way to her toes. "Nothing's going to happen to me. I'll be back. We'll talk. Promise."

Then he kissed her hard, his tongue sliding against hers all too briefly before he pushed her away.

It was time to go to work. Dane deliberately walked away as the assault boat made contact with the trawler. Ivy called after him, but he couldn't look back. He knew she was pissed that she was being offloaded along with Miguel Ruiz, but he couldn't fix that.

Her job was taking Ruiz in. His job was stopping this submarine before it put a nuke in terrorist hands on US soil. As the trawler's engines spooled up, Dane dared a look. Ivy was at the rail, clutching it with both hands, the light from the trawler shining on her face.

He had the craziest thought that he might not ever see her again. That this was the end and they'd said and done all they would ever do together.

He turned away again, determined not to look back. The assault boat sped into the night, and the Coast Guard trawler headed toward shore. Matt and Billy the Kid were looking at the computer console. Then Matt looked over at Dane.

"Your team's in position, Viking. Lieutenant JG Marchand wants to speak to you." Matt grinned then. "A fellow Cajun boy. I like this guy."

Dane waited for Billy to patch the call into his headset. The comm link crackled and then Remy's voice came over the air.

"Ghost One awaiting your orders, sir. And it's damn good to hear from you. Thought you'd bugged out and went to join the Army."

Dane snorted. "Goddamn, Remy Marchand, it's good to hear from you too. If I didn't already know you'd take it the wrong way, I'd kiss your pretty face the next time we meet."

"Always knew you wanted me, sir."

"Yeah, I want you all right. I want you and the guys to help HOT get these fuckers tonight. We can't let this damn thing get by us."

"Sir…" Remy sounded just a little hesitant, and Dane figured he knew what was coming next. "HOT exists? This isn't some joke between admirals yanking our chain?"

Dane looked at the men standing on the boat with him. They were big, badass motherfuckers who didn't do any of this for the glory of it. Hell, they didn't even get any glory because no one knew they existed. SEAL Team Six were the ones typically in the news, the ones who got credit for taking down high-profile terrorists like Bin Laden. And yet HOT was there too, quietly working in the background, eliminating the kind of terrorists who wanted to leave an even bigger mark on the world than Bin Laden had.

He'd come into this with a chip on his shoulder for the Army and its brass. But Colonel Mendez, for all his autocratic ways—and yeah, that's how a commander was supposed to be—cared about giving his people the best tools for the job. He also cared about everyone under his command, not just the mission. The fact he'd sent them after Ivy when there was so much at stake said a lot for the man.

Dane couldn't help but respect that kind of dedication.

"Yeah, they exist," he said. "Even better, you're now a part of them."

Had he just said "even better"? Yeah, he fucking had. And he meant it. Because HOT was exciting and different, and he realized he was looking forward to being a part of the organization. Leading the first SEAL team to be assigned to HOT. It was a helluva challenge—and he loved challenges.

"Heard that too. Didn't want to believe it until you gave the word." Remy huffed a breath. "All right, we're ready. Waiting for your command."

Dane glanced at his dive watch. "ETA in ten."

"We'll be here."

"I know you will, you ornery Cajun motherfucker. Can't wait to see you."

"Easy does it, sir. I'm spoken for."

Dane laughed. Remy was spoken for all right—by every woman he met. "So am I, man. But we'll make it work somehow."

TWENTY-SIX

IN THE END, THE OP was textbook. Or as textbook as it could be for a situation they'd never encountered before. The sub surfaced about a mile from shore. *Bad Medicine* was waiting, the men chattering excitedly with no idea there was a SEAL team beneath the waves.

HOT pulled into position and waited for the signal from Dane's SEALs. Remy and his team were using submersibles to power through the water quietly. Their goal was to disable the rotors on *Bad Medicine* and the rudder on the sub. They would also sabotage the planes in order to prevent the sub from submerging once the fighting started. If the submarine went under, there was a chance the terrorists would blow the warhead where they were. It wouldn't do the kind of damage that trucking the missile to Tampa—or any port—would do, but a nuclear bomb going off this close to shore would definitely cause damage to a very wide swath of Florida.

Dane listened intently on his comm link. He was calm because he was always calm during a mission, but the adrenaline flowed hot and fast. He wanted to be beneath the waves with his guys but he had to content himself with monitoring their progress from the assault boat.

He looked up at the faces trained on his. They were tense, waiting. Once they got the all clear from Remy, they were throttling this motherfucker up and taking the fight to the tangos. There was still a danger with the missile, but the nuclear launch sequence took time to perform—and HOT wasn't giving these assholes the time to detonate their weapon, assuming they had the correct launch codes in the first place.

"Moby Dick is in the net," Remy said, his voice quiet and sure in the night. "And he ain't getting away."

"Copy that," Dane said. "Captain Ahab coming in for the kill."

Chase took them so close to the two enemy craft without alerting the tangos that Dane could see the expressions on the men's faces without needing binoculars.

"We're a go," Matt said. "Let's put this bitch to bed."

The lights on the assault boat suddenly switched on, flooding the area—and the enemies—with enough candle-power to light up the Superdome. The men scrambled for their weapons, but they were too blind to hit anything. Two men shimmied down the hatch of the sub, but before they could shut it, a wetsuit-clad SEAL was there, shouting orders and taking prisoners.

Dane stormed *Bad Medicine* with three of the guys. They gathered up the men—Omar Baz and the others who'd been prepared to betray their adopted country—and hustled them over to the assault boat where they were blindfolded and cuffed before being stowed in the hold.

The men who'd been piloting the submarine were captured and trussed as well. Dane and Matt transferred over to the submarine and went down the hatch. The sub wasn't big, but it was roomier than was typical for a drug-running sub. It had compartments for drugs, and it was lined with over two hundred batteries for power. It also stank like ten-day-old jock straps.

"And there it is," Matt said. "The source of all the trouble."

A fat, camouflage-painted missile took up a good portion of the sub, looking like anything but a weapon capable of destroying thousands of lives.

"How'd they get this sonofabitch on board?" Dane said, looking at the missile and then up at the hatch. "That was a feat."

Before Matt could answer, there was a scraping noise from one of the compartments—and then the door flung upward and an armed man took aim at the nearest target he could find.

The gunshot cracked like a sonic boom in the small space.

Ivy slouched in a chair next to Ace's bed. The hospital hadn't wanted to let her in at first, but she'd called Leslie Webb, who'd had a nice little chat with the administrator about who was family. So now she was here, holding Ace's hand and waiting for him to wake up. Tears pricked her eyes as she watched him breathe with the help of a ventilator.

"He was lucky," the nurse said as she checked his vitals. "The bullet didn't hit anything major, but he lost a lot of blood. If he hadn't been in as good shape as he is, he might not have made it."

Ivy gave the woman a watery smile. "Ace loves to work out. Never saw a man more obsessed with keeping fit."

"Well, honey, it shows. He's kinda gorgeous, you know?"

"He is."

The nurse left her then, and Ivy laid her cheek against Ace's hand. "You need to wake up, buddy. We've got work to do."

But Ace didn't stir, and Ivy swallowed a load of frustration and fear. She still hadn't heard from Dane, and it had been hours since she'd been hustled off the HOT assault boat and onto a Coast Guard vessel.

Miguel Ruiz was in custody, charged with kidnapping a federal officer and attempted murder of another. No matter how many high-powered lawyers he brought in, he wasn't getting out of the US. Ivy wanted to be in on his interrogation, but that wasn't going to happen. She'd told Leslie about the family connection, though she would have preferred to go to her grave with that information.

But she had to share it before Miguel did even though it effectively meant she was off the case. No more Ruiz takedowns for her. Though she'd gotten the big boss and he wasn't going anywhere, so maybe she'd gotten a little justice for her mother after all. She'd wanted to kill him, but maybe this was better. This way he could detail his networks and give the DEA the information they needed to put an end to the Ruiz branch of the drug trade.

She had no doubt he would bargain. He would have to if he didn't want to end up in a maximum-security facility. No, he'd want the country-club experience—and they'd give it to him if he helped them take down his family.

Her phone—a new one that had been waiting for her when she reached Miami—buzzed in her pocket. She snatched it up and answered with a clipped "McGill."

She could hear the wind. And then a voice spoke.

"We got them. Wanted you to know."

A boat motor churned in the background, and Ivy's insides turned to mush. "Dane? You're okay?"

"Calling you, aren't I?"

"Yes." She noticed that he sounded strained, but she supposed that was because he'd just come off a high-pressure mission. She knew what it was like to stay keyed up afterward. "How did you know about this number?"

"Mendez."

Thank you, Colonel Mendez. "When will I see you?"

"We're on the way home. Have to debrief. See you in a few days."

"Days?" That wasn't what she'd expected, and it made her chest hurt. What would happen to their conversation in a few days? He'd seemed to care earlier, and yet... what if he didn't care the way she wanted him to? What if she was completely wrong about everything?

"It's the job, baby. You know that."

"Yes, I know." It was one of the things that had torn them apart in the first place—but what if it was more than that this time? What if he was looking for a way out, no matter that he'd called her his girl earlier? Could that have simply been a knee-jerk response?

Her heart throbbed with pain and questions and uncertainty, yet there would be no answers tonight.

"How's Ace?"

She glanced at her partner. "Still in a coma."

"I'm sorry, honey. But he's tough. He'll pull through. The doctors said so."

"I know."

There were voices in the background. "Gotta go, Ivy. Talk to you in DC."

She gripped the phone tight. This wasn't how she wanted it to end. But what could she say? I love you?

No, not going there. Not like this.

"Okay. See you later."

"Yeah, see you."

The phone went dead, and she cradled it against her cheek, numbness slipping through her in time to the beeping of Ace's machines.

Everything in her life was changing, and she had no control. Her partner was in a coma. The job she'd loved for years was in jeopardy. She wasn't even *who* she'd thought she was all these years—and the ex-husband she'd tried so hard to forget was once more at the center of her thoughts. The center of her world.

Ivy dropped her head to the bar on Ace's bed and closed her eyes. What more could go wrong?

TWENTY-SEVEN

DANE TUGGED AT HIS COLLAR and thought for at least the millionth time that this was a bad idea. He probably should have called first.

But it was too late now. He'd donned the Navy whites, complete with his SEAL trident and all his medals over his left pocket. He stared at his mirrored reflection in the elevator. Damn, would he impress her or scare her? He knew he looked good in the whites, but his eye was black and blue, the edges of the bruise yellowing. When that tango had surprised them in the hold of the sub, he'd gone down hard, hitting his face against the steel bench and practically knocking himself out.

Matt hadn't fared much better. He'd sprained his wrist and scraped the hell out of his hand. The bullet the asshole had fired at them ricocheted off the steel two or three times before hitting the assailant in the throat. It was divine justice, but damn if it hadn't been a scary few seconds.

They'd hauled the fucker out of the sub, bleeding profusely from his wound, and secured the cargo. The missile was safely tucked away in a military bunker, its guts being disassembled and studied. Florida would never know what had almost happened to it, thank God.

Dane held a bouquet of white and pink tulips in his left hand—because tulips were Ivy's favorite—and felt the heat of uncertainty crawling up his throat again. Maybe he shouldn't have gotten Colonel Mendez to get him entry into the DEA. Maybe he should have gone to her apartment and waited for her like a sensible man.

But he didn't want to wait, and he didn't want to do anything by half measures. Because the one thing he'd realized during this mission was that he wanted Ivy back in his life. However she would take him. When he'd thought he'd lost her—Jesus, he couldn't even think about it. That had been the lowest moment of his life.

The elevator opened, and he found himself on the floor that was supposed to be where Ivy worked. He strode into the foyer and found a receptionist whose mouth dropped open as he approached.

"Oh, uh, can I help you, sir?"

"Ivy McGill," he said. "I'm here to see her."

"I, uh… yes, sir." She picked up the phone and dialed. After a few moments, she frowned at him. "Agent McGill isn't at her desk, sir."

Frustration hammered him. "How about Leslie Webb?"

"Of course, sir." She dialed again. This time someone must have answered because she started to talk. "Yes, ma'am. A Navy man, ma'am. In whites, yes. Holding flowers."

When she hung up, she stood. "This way, sir."

She led him through doors that opened into a cube

farm. He followed her through the aisles until she reached a group of desks. A woman looked up, interest crossing her features as she stood.

"Who's this, Megan?" she asked the receptionist.

Dane held out his hand. "Lieutenant Erikson, ma'am. Pleased to meet you."

The woman's eyes roved over him as she took his hand and shook it. "Agent Taylor. Can we help you, Lieutenant?"

"Only if you know where Agent McGill is."

"Uh, I think she went down the hall for a few minutes. Probably checking on something." Her gaze landed on his chest. "You're a SEAL."

"Yes, ma'am."

"Dane?"

He swung around to find Ivy approaching. Her mouth dropped open, her pretty eyes growing wide and a maybe even a little surprised. And then there was the concern when she took in his bruised face. She put a hand to her mouth and didn't say a word.

"Hello, Ivy," he said as warmth flowed through him like a hot shower on a cold day.

"I… Dane, are you all right?"

"Fine… why?"

She shook her head. "That's a hell of a shiner."

"Got into a little scrape."

"A little scrape." Her throat worked, and then her gaze dropped over him, back up again. "Are you on your way to a military banquet or something?"

He grinned. "Said I wanted to talk to you."

She crossed her arms and a little current of dread zipped through him. In truth, he had no idea what kind of reception she was going to give him. Maybe his heart was the only one pounding like crazy. Maybe he was the only one who thought he might die if he didn't get to kiss her again.

"It's been nearly two weeks since I last heard from you. I thought you'd changed your mind."

Changed his mind? No way. "It's been ten days. And I've been busy, Ivy. After action reports, moving me and my team to DC from Virginia Beach, getting briefed at the new job."

It sounded lame, he knew, but the truth was that moving an entire SEAL team to DC took time and effort. They were a part of HOT now, and he didn't mind that at all. Surprisingly.

His father, even more surprisingly, was proud as a peacock. The general knew about HOT—and he'd nearly busted his buttons over the idea his son was leading the first SEAL team under HOT's direction. It was definitely a departure from their usual encounters. Dane didn't imagine that meant they were suddenly going to be chummy-chummy, but maybe it was the beginning of something.

Just like he hoped this was the beginning of something.

"You could have called," Ivy said.

He could have. He heard the hurt in her voice and thought maybe he should have. But the days had been packed and he'd only returned to the area this morning. "What I need to say has to be said in person."

"All right."

Dane held out the flowers. "You love tulips."

It took her a moment, but she reached for them. "I do. Thank you."

Dane swore beneath his breath. He couldn't do this polite back-and-forth bullshit, working his way up to the point while watching her face for signs of anger or sadness or hopelessness. Not when his heart felt like it might burst out of his chest because it hammered so hard for her. "Ivy, for God's sake, I missed you."

He thought her eyes grew a little misty. "It's only been a few days."

He shook his head. "No. I *missed* you. For four and a half years. Dumbest thing I ever did was give up on us."

People stood and stared over their cubicles now. But he didn't care. He had things to say, and he didn't care who heard them. The floodgates banged open on their hinges.

"I, uh… I missed you too."

He blinked. "You did?"

"Yes, I did. Why else would I fall into bed with you after not seeing you for so long?"

"Oh my," someone said.

"You go, girl," someone else said.

"Hell yeah," another voice offered.

"I'd fall into bed with that," a male voice replied, and Dane looked up to find Ace hobbling down another aisle with a cane. He looked a bit strained, a bit pale. But he was alive, and that was a good thing. He'd saved Ivy's life, whether he believed it or not. Without Max, Ruiz would have gotten to Ivy another way—and maybe they wouldn't have found her in time.

"Thanks, dude. I appreciate that," Dane said, reaching out to shake Ace's hand. The other man grinned as if he hadn't expected such a response—but then he shook Dane's hand with a strong grip, even if it wasn't quite as strong as it had once been.

"Eh, just trying to help."

"You are *not* helping, Ace," Ivy said. "Now sit down and shut up."

"Honey, I was making sure you didn't continue the conversation without me. I *got* to hear this."

Ivy helped him into his chair even though he fussed at her not to do it. When he was settled, she patted him on the shoulder and then wheeled him a little closer to Dane.

Dane wanted to laugh. Instead, he watched Ivy and thought how much he loved this damn woman. She cared about people, and she was brave and loyal. She wasn't perfect, but then neither was he. They had plenty to work out, but this time he was determined to try. Because he needed her. He knew that now. Pride had gotten in the way before. Pride and fear—and he wasn't letting them win this time.

"I want to try again, Ivy. We can take it slow if you want. I'll ask you out. We can date, take our time. Maybe we'll spend the night together in a couple of months or so. See how that goes."

She was staring at him like he'd spoken Klingon or something. Then she laughed. "I'm sorry… take our time? Since when has that ever worked for us? And if you think I'm waiting two months to go to bed with you again, you are *so* wrong. What kind of man shows up looking like"— she waved a hand up and down his body—"*that* and says we're going to take it slow?"

His heart thudded hard. A hot wave of possession curled inside his gut, urging him to claim her. He held out his hand. He didn't say a word. She stared at it for a long moment.

"If you don't leap into that man's arms, I'm doing it

for you," Ace grumbled.

Ivy laughed—and then she reached out and took Dane's hand. He didn't know what she thought he might do, but he wasn't one for half measures. He tugged her to him and then swept her up and into his arms. She gasped when her feet left the ground. And then she buried her head against his neck and laughed softly.

"What is this, Dane? What has gotten into you?"

"Romance, honey. This is romance."

She tilted her head and caressed his cheek while her officemates cheered. "This is crazy," she whispered.

"I know, baby," he whispered back. "But that's how I feel. Crazy for you. I love you, Ivy. I've always loved you."

She sniffled. "I love you too, Dane. I never stopped."

"Hallelujah," he said. He stared at her fiercely. "It's going to work this time, babe. We aren't giving up. This is too precious not to fight for."

"I know that," she said softly. And then she pressed her lips to his, and everything felt right.

EPILOGUE

IVY ROLLED OVER IN BED and found Dane propped on an elbow, watching her.

"What?" she asked, yawning. She was tired but happy. What a night.

"Nothing." He slid a finger down her arm and smiled. "I like looking at you."

"More than looking, if last night was any indication."

He laughed. "Oh yeah, more than looking."

She slid her arms around his neck and arched into him. "That was a cheap shot, wearing your whites. No woman can say no to a man in Navy whites."

"That's what I was counting on." He grinned and waggled his eyebrows.

She pressed her body to his, naked skin to naked skin. Oh, that felt so nice. He hadn't put her down yesterday. He'd told Ace she was taking the rest of the day off, then he'd carried her outside and put her in his car. He'd driven her to the house he'd rented in suburban Maryland, and then he'd carried her up the steps and straight to the bedroom. There, he'd performed the sexiest striptease any woman had ever been treated to before worshipping her body with his hands and mouth and bringing her to orgasm again and again.

To say Ivy was sated was an understatement. But she wasn't oblivious. She carefully traced her fingers over the bruising on his face.

"How did you get this black eye?"

Dane looked up from where he'd been pressing his lips to her throat. "Some asshole fired at Matt and me in the sub. We hit the deck—and I hit steel."

Ivy swallowed. "I'm going to pretend you didn't say anything about someone firing at you."

He squeezed her. "Yeah, well you scared the shit out of me when you attacked Ruiz, so maybe we're even."

Ivy dropped her gaze and studied his chest. She hadn't told him everything yet. The words were still hard to say. "My mother was a Ruiz," she said softly, her throat hurting. "Miguel is my uncle. He tried to rape me, Dane."

Dane crushed her to him. "Oh honey. Shit."

She sniffed. "It's okay. Nothing happened because you and your guys showed up… but he killed my mother."

He tilted her head back and searched her gaze. "I thought she died of a drug overdose."

"She did, but she was smuggling drugs in her stomach. One of the packets broke. I never told you that part because I was ashamed. I felt like it was my fault."

He brushed her hair from her face. "How could it be your fault, Ivy? You were a kid."

This was the part that hurt. "She wanted a better life for us. She went back to her family in hopes of getting that life."

Dane looked angry. "Yeah, and her fucking brother

forced her to do something dangerous. That's not your fault."

"I know." She tongued his pec and he shuddered beneath her lips. "I felt guilty for a long time, but I'm working on it."

"You can't be blamed for any of it, Ivy. Your father leaving, your mother smuggling drugs—none of it is your fault, do you understand? If they had been thinking of you at all, they wouldn't have fucking done *any* of it."

Warmth and belonging flowed through her like hot honey. "You're so good to me. Good *for* me. I love you, Dane."

His hands skimmed down her sides, leaving a trail of goose bumps in their wake.

"I won't leave you, Ivy. You mean too much to me. I'd take a bullet for you."

She shuddered. "I hope it never comes to that. Something happened to me in Florida... I realized how empty my life has been without you in it. As much as you terrify me, as much as you confuse me—nothing is better than when we're together."

He kissed her long and hard, until she was hot and melting in his arms. And then he rolled her beneath him and entered her in one long thrust. Ivy moaned with pleasure. They began to move together, bodies and breaths mingling, heartbeats in tune, until she couldn't hold back the tide any longer. She came in a rush, crying his name as her body splintered into a million tiny pieces.

Life was complete with this man. Unpredictable and a touch frightening, but complete.

"We're going to make it this time," he said after they'd recovered.

She traced a finger over the glistening muscles of his chest. "We're still in very demanding jobs. Are you certain you're okay with that?"

The smile he gave her made her heart ache. "I am. But I'll leave the Navy for you, Ivy, if you want me to. I have to finish out my commitment, but I'll leave when it's over."

She put a hand over his mouth. Did she want that? Sure, part of her did. But loving Dane was trusting Dane. Letting him go and knowing he'd return. Letting him be who he was and supporting him.

"No, you won't. You're a SEAL."

"I don't have to be—"

"Yes, you do. And I understand that."

"God, I love you. So fucking much."

She laughed. "I know. I really do know it, Dane. I'm not scared anymore."

"There's nothing to be scared of. I've got your back. Always."

"And I've got yours." She pushed her fingers through his hair. He'd cut it since she'd last seen him, but she thought even if he was bald he'd be sexy. "But there's only one requirement."

His brows drew together. "What's that?"

"You have to wear those Navy whites at least once a month."

"Honey, if you strip me out of them, I'll wear them every day."

Ivy laughed. "Deal."

ABOUT THE AUTHOR

LYNN RAYE HARRIS is the *New York Times* and *USA Today* bestselling author of the HOSTILE OPERATIONS TEAM SERIES of military romances as well as 20 books for Harlequin Presents. A former finalist for the Romance Writers of America's Golden Heart Award and the National Readers Choice Award, Lynn lives in Alabama with her handsome former military husband and two crazy cats. Lynn's books have been called "exceptional and emotional," "intense," and "sizzling." Lynn's books have sold over 2 million copies worldwide.

Connect with me online:
Facebook: https://www.facebook.com/AuthorLynnRayeHarris
Twitter: https://twitter.com/LynnRayeHarris
Website: http://www.LynnRayeHarris.com
Newsletter: http://bit.ly/LRHNews
Email: Lynn@LynnRayeHarris.com

Join my Hostile Operations Team Readers and Fans Group
on Facebook:
https://www.facebook.com/groups/HOTReadersAndFans/

14373125R00108

Printed in Great Britain
by Amazon.co.uk, Ltd.,
Marston Gate.